Two decades ago, un...
the New York Ti...
this macho...

PRAISE FOR RANDY WAYNE WHITE
AND HIS NOVELS

"What James Lee Burke has done for Louisiana, Tony Hillerman for the Southwest, John Sandford for Minnesota, and Joe R. Lansdale for east Texas, Randy Wayne White does for his own little acre."
—*Chicago Tribune*

"White takes us places that no other Florida mystery writer can hope to find." —Carl Hiaasen

"White brings vivid imagination to his fight scenes. Think Mickey Spillane meets *The Matrix*."
—*People*

"A major new talent . . . hits the ground running . . . a virtually perfect piece of work. He's the best new writer we've encountered since Carl Hiaasen." —*The Denver Post*

"White is the rightful heir to joining John D. Mac-Donald, Carl Hiaasen, James Hall, Geoffrey Norman. . . . His precise prose is as fresh and pungent as a salty breeze." —*The Tampa Tribune*

"White doesn't just use Florida as a backdrop, but he also makes the smell, sound, and physicality of the state leap off the page."
—*South Florida Sun-Sentinel*

continued . . .

"This satisfying madcap fare could go seismic on the regional bestseller lists." —*Publishers Weekly*

"He describes southwestern Florida so well it's easy to smell the salt tang in the air and feel the cool gulf breeze. —*Mansfield News Journal*

The
DEEP SIX

Randy Wayne White
writing as Randy Striker

A SIGNET BOOK

SIGNET
Published by New American Library, a division of
Penguin Group (USA) Inc., 375 Hudson Street,
New York, New York 10014, USA
Penguin Group (Canada), 90 Eglinton Avenue East, Suite 700, Toronto,
Ontario M4P 2Y3, Canada (a division of Pearson Penguin Canada Inc.)
Penguin Books Ltd., 80 Strand, London WC2R 0RL, England
Penguin Ireland, 25 St. Stephen's Green, Dublin 2,
Ireland (a division of Penguin Books Ltd.)
Penguin Group (Australia), 250 Camberwell Road, Camberwell, Victoria 3124,
Australia (a division of Pearson Australia Group Pty. Ltd.)
Penguin Books India Pvt. Ltd., 11 Community Centre, Panchsheel Park,
New Delhi - 110 017, India
Penguin Group (NZ), cnr Airborne and Rosedale Roads, Albany,
Auckland 1310, New Zealand (a division of Pearson New Zealand Ltd.)
Penguin Books (South Africa) (Pty.) Ltd., 24 Sturdee Avenue,
Rosebank, Johannesburg 2196, South Africa

Penguin Books Ltd., Registered Offices:
80 Strand, London WC2R 0RL, England

Published by Signet, an imprint of New American Library,
a division of Penguin Group (USA) Inc.

First Printing, February 1981
First Printing (Author Introduction), October 2006
10 9 8 7 6 5 4 3 2 1

For my friends Dr. Harold Westervelt,
Bob Fizer, Dr. Amanda Evans, and
dear Roberta Petish

Introduction

In the winter of 1980, I received a surprising phone call from an editor at Signet Books—surprising because, as a Florida fishing guide, the only time New Yorkers called me was to charter my boat. And if any of my clients were editors, they were savvy enough not to admit it.

The editor said she'd read a story by me in *Outside Magazine* and was impressed. Did I have time to talk?

As a mediocre high school jock, my idols were writers, not ball players. I had a dream job as a light-tackle guide, yet I was still obsessed with my own dream of writing for a living. For years, before and after charters, I'd worked hard at the craft. Selling a story to *Outside*, one of the country's finest publications, was a huge break. I was about to finish a novel, but this was the first time New York had called.

Yes, I had time to talk.

The editor, whose name was Joanie, told me Signet wanted to launch a paperback thriller series that featured a recurring he-man hero. "We want at least four writers on the project because we want to keep the books coming, publishing one right after the other, to create momentum."

Four writers producing books with the same character?

"Characters," Joanie corrected. "Once we get going, the cast will become standard."

Signet already had a template for the hero. He was a Vietnam vet turned Key West fishing guide, she said, talking as if the man existed. He was surfer-boy blond, and he'd been friends with Hemingway.

I am not a literary historian, but all my instincts told me the timetable seemed problematic. I said nothing.

"He has a shark scar," Joanie added, "and he's freakishly strong. Like a man who lifts weights all the time."

The guys I knew who lifted weights were also freakishly clumsy, so . . . maybe the hero, while visiting a local aquarium, tripped during feeding time?

My brain was already problem-solving.

"He lives in Key West," she said, "so, of course, he has to be an expert on the area. That's why I'm calling. You live in Key West, and I liked your magazine story a lot. It seems like a natural fit."

Actually, I fished out of Sanibel Island, on Florida's Gulf Coast, a six hour drive from Sloppy Joe's, but this was no time for petty details.

"Have you ever been to Key West?" I asked the editor. "Great sunsets."

Editors, I have since learned, can also be cagey. Joanie didn't offer me the job. She had already settled on three of the four writers, she said, but if I was willing to submit a few sample chapters on speculation, she'd give me serious consideration.

Money? A contract? That stuff was "all standard," she told me, and could be discussed later.

"I'll warn you right now," she said, "there are a couple of other writers we're considering, so you need to get at least three chapters to me within a month. Then I'll let you know."

I hung up the phone, stunned by my good fortune. My first son, Lee, had been born only a few months earlier. My much adored wife, Debra, and I were desperate for money because the weather that winter had been miserable for fishing. But it was *perfect* for writing.

I went to my desk, determined not to let my young family down.

At Tarpon Bay Marina, where I was a guide, my friend Ralph Woodring owned a boat with *Dusky* painted in big blue letters on the side. My friend, Graeme Mellor, lived on a Morgan sailboat named *No Mas*.

Dusky MacMorgan was born.

Every winter, Clyde Beatty-Cole Bros. Circus came to town. Their trapeze artists, I realized, were not only freakishly strong, but they were also freakishly nimble.

Dusky gathered depth.

One of my best friends was the late Dr. Harold Westervelt, a gifted orthopedic surgeon. Dr. Westervelt became the Edison of Death, and he loved introducing himself that way to new patients. His son, David, became Westy O'Davis, and our spearfishing pal, Billy, became Billy Mack.

Problems with my hero's shark scar and his devoted friendship with Hemingway were also solved.

Working around the clock, pounding away at my

old black manual typewriter, I wrote *Key West Connection* in nine days. On a Monday morning, I waited for the post office to open to send it to New York.

Joanie sounded a little dazed when she telephoned on Friday. Was I willing to try a second book on spec?

Hell, yes.

God, I was beginning to *love* New York's can-do attitude.

The other three writers (if they ever existed) were fired, and I became the sole proprietor of Captain Dusky MacMorgan—although Signet owned the copyright and all other rights after I signed Joanie's "standard" contract. (This injustice was later made right by a willing and steadfast publisher and my brilliant agent.)

If Joanie (a fine editor) feels badly about that today, she shouldn't. I would've signed for less.

I wrote seven of what I would come to refer to as "duck and fuck" books because in alternating chapters Dusky would duck a few bullets, then spend much-deserved time alone with a heroine.

Seldom did a piece of paper go into my old typewriter that was ripped out and thrown away, and I suspect that's the way the books read. I don't know. I've never reread them. I do remember using obvious clichés, a form of self-loathing, as if to remind myself that I should be doing my *own* writing, not this job-of-work.

The book you are now holding, and the other six, constituted a training arena for a young writer who took seriously the discipline demanded by his craft and also the financial imperatives of being a young father.

For years, I apologized for these books. I no longer do.

—Randy Wayne White
Cartagena, Colombia

1

Underwater, in the angling tawny light of late afternoon, everything was gold. Flaxen sea fans undulated in the current that swept around the reef, and aureated and jewel-crested reef fish watched the naked woman as she reached beneath a pod of brain coral and pulled out a spiny lobster. It was a big one—enough for her half of the supper we would eat back on my thirty-four-foot cruiser, the *Sniper.* Drifting above, mask in the water, breathing easily through my snorkel, I watched the naked woman with delight. Even she appeared gold in that strange afternoon light; a tenuous light that seems unique to the open sea, and to the reef islands far, far off Key West. It is a light that does more than illuminate—it seems to melt and liquefy, gilding everything it touches: the Australian pines and coconut palms that leaned in windward strands on nearby Fullmoon Cay; the long sweep of white beach on Marquesas Keys; the blue and then orange expanse of open sea as the sun whirled toward dusk, setting behind the

Dry Tortugas. And the woman, too. Drifting
above the reef, I watched her slow ascent. Her
blond hair streamed behind her in a long veil.
After a month on my boat, her body was bronzed
and trim, and the bikini strips on chest and hips
appeared as pale geometries upon her golden nakedness. She winked at me as she stroked toward
the surface, holding the lobster like a prize.

Gold, gold, gold.

Later, it would return in my memory as a
prophecy. An augury of the future. That's the way
our minds work. Something happens, and our
brains scan the past for omens. It's a human com-
pulsion: search for order in a universe that, at
times, seems to be anything but orderly. A friend
dies and, in our minds, his last words take on
portentous significance. We are involved in an accident, and we remember that "something" told
us not to take the trip. Now it was golden light
on a golden sea and in less than two hours it
would take on a whole new meaning.

I watched the girl. She wore only mask, fins and
snorkel. Oxygen bubbles, clinging to her blond tri-
angle of body hair, looked like little pearls, and
her breasts moved with heavy, liquid weight. Her
beauty, the reef, and the afternoon light filled me
with a strange yearning.

"Hey! Look what I've got!" She pulled the mask
off her perfect face, laughing with delight.

"I know what you've got—it's hard to miss."

She slapped at me with mock outrage. "Oh,
you! I'm talking about the lobster. Isn't he a
beauty?"

He was indeed. A beautiful crustacean, the Flor-

ida lobster. No claws, but with sharp spines between their eyes that can needle through heavy
cotton gloves. And because of that, this woman,
Lisa-lee Johnson—Lee, I called her—hadn't caught
one the whole trip. But she wasn't one to give up.
Some afternoons she would come back from diving with her hands perforated, then sneak off to
the first-aid kit to doctor herself in private. She
never complained and I never let on that I knew.
And the next day she would go back for more.
Until now. Finally, she had caught one. And it
was a beaut. A two-pounder, easy. Her blue eyes
gleamed victoriously as she dropped it, squeaking
and kicking, into my dive bag, and we swam together over to the little Boston Whaler I had
hauled along behind my *Sniper.*

"And what about your supper?" She sat naked
on the low gunnel of the thirteen-foot boat, her
blond hair hanging down in a thick wet rope,
dripping water on her upturned breasts.

"Ah . . . supper . . . oh, yeah. . . ."

"Your mind seems to be someplace else,
Dusky." She grinned bawdily.

"Dressed the way you are, woman, I find that
my thoughts are on anything but food."

The smile left her face, and a new look came
into her blue eyes; a heavy, sleepy look with
which I had become very familiar over the past
month. It had been a good month. A month of
sun and fish and clear water; a month of aimless
cruising and, then, love. In our own ways, we
were both healing. Lee had separated from her
domineering husband. And for me, only two eternal months before, the pirates, the ruthless ones,

the money-hungry drug runners, had blown my life apart. A little ignition bomb in the trunk of our old blue Chevy. How were they to know that I wouldn't be the one to start it that awful August night? And why should they care that my beautiful wife, Janet, and my twin boys, Ernest and Honor, had been killed instead?

Well, I had made them care. And the few I had allowed to live would regret it until their own dying day.

So, when I was done with them, I had returned to my dock in Key West to find this woman, Lisa-lee Johnson. I had come to know and admire her when she and her husband chartered me and my *Sniper* for a day of fishing, and I had welcomed her tearful request to cruise alone for a few weeks. She wanted to cruise to think. And I wanted to get away so I wouldn't have to think. When we left Key West and headed across Florida Bay, we were two strangers filled with our own private horrors. The first week had been one of nervous laughter and averted glances. Neither of us was interested in love—just companionship. I had seen too much recent death and had done too much killing to want to be alone. And she—well, she seemed to be looking for a man strong enough not to try to hurry her into the sack; a man she could talk to and depend upon while she made up her mind about the husband she had left behind.

But it seemed inevitable that we would become lovers. I had known from our first meeting that there was a strong sexual awareness between us. You know it instinctively, and it has nothing to do with coy exchanges and suggestive remarks.

And when we had finally kissed, it was like a dam breaking. We couldn't get each other's clothes off fast enough. We couldn't touch each other enough. We couldn't satisfy each other enough.

"Oh, Dusky, is it so awful that I want you this way . . . ?"

"No, Lee. No. . . ."

It was an affirmation of the things we had left behind; an affirmation of the new lives each of us would have to find. And afterward, we would talk: long, rambling, self-indulgent conversations, telling each other everything. We didn't talk like lovers—nothing about our combined plans and hopes for the future. We talked like best friends. We soothed each other and tried to bolster sagging egos and shattered dreams.

It was harder for me to talk than it was for Lee. I find it difficult to stick more than four words into a sentence, and more than one sentence into a paragraph. I've always been quiet. Not shy, just quiet. My wife used to kid me by calling me Captain Stoic. But finally, with Lee's gentle help, the words started pouring out. When someone you love dies, you first feel outrage, then remorse, then guilt. I had been through the remorse and outrage—nearly a dozen men died in the flare of it. And Lee had helped me reason the guilt away.

"I just can't figure out the why of it. Why did that woman and those two boys have to die?"

"Dusky, you told me once when we first met that for some things there are no reasonable explanations. There is only acceptance. It's happened. Accept it. And go on."

So we had worked our way across Florida Bay,

up into the Ten Thousand Islands wilderness on the mainland west coast, and then back across open ocean to the Dry Tortugas, and then here, to the Marquesas, working our way along to Key West and the end of the trip. The autumn days were hot and calm; perfect days for slow love and cold beer and talk; golden autumn days.

Golden.

Lee sat on the gunnel of the Boston Whaler, her long legs draping over into the clear water. And when her eyes softened, I leaned and kissed her, tasting the salt on her lips, feeling the warmth of her mix with the warm seawind that wafted across Fullmoon Cay to the reef over which our little boat was anchored.

"And what about your supper, Captain?" She smiled at me impishly. I was close enough to her face to see the little bronze flecks in her blue eyes.

"I've got my sling. I'll go down and shoot a snapper—later."

"Later?" She smiled and kissed me.

"Later."

Naked, she stretched back on the mahogany seat of the Whaler, her eyes closed, her arms folded behind her head.

"You're cold from diving."

"Hum . . . so I see."

A bottle of coconut oil sat on the little console, warm from its day in the sun. "This might help." I began to massage it into her skin, enjoying the scent of it, and the vision of this lovely blond woman.

"You seem to be concentrating on limited areas, Captain."

"Certain parts of you look colder than others."

She opened one eye, squinting at me. "And parts of you look anything but cold."

I put down the coconut oil and leaned over her, kissing her body, caressing her outstretched legs, feeling her breasts full against me, and then—and then she pushed me away, giggling vampishly. "Your turn to suffer, MacMorgan!"

"What?"

Oh, she made me suffer. With the coconut oil. And her hands. And her lips. And had she made me suffer a minute more, I would have attacked her then and there. But she didn't. Instead, she grabbed one of the yellow Dacor scuba tanks and her mask and, with a short laugh, jumped into the clear water. And I soon followed.

Beside the reef was a pocket of sand. Iridescent blue-and-green parrot fish scurried away at our approach, and the woman lay back in the sand, motioning for me. And then, three fathoms down, we made slow love. Beneath clear water, experimenting with the new weightlessness and the variations it allowed, we coupled in a stream of bubbles, drifting with the sea. Barracuda looked on, stern as maidenly aunts, and yellow-eyed groupers peered at us strangely from their rocky hideaways. I was filled with my passion for Lee and my love of the sea, but I also felt a sweet-sad ache, because I knew that she would be leaving me upon our return to Key West, and that I would probably never see her again.

Afterward, Lee climbed back on the little Whaler to bask in the sun and I took my sling

down to the reef alone. I wore no tank. Even after
three tours of duty in Nam as a Navy SEAL, I still
preferred just mask and fins. No regulator to
worry about. No metal fittings to konk you on the
back of the head. When I am in the water I love
the freedom of unhampered motion. Besides,
spearfishing with a tank is one of the most pathetically unfair "sports" imaginable. The poor fish
doesn't have a chance. I dove down to the top of
the reef, then worked my way along a shelf of
coral in about twenty feet of water. Small snapper
and yellowtail moved away from me in perfect,
orderly sheets, as if one mind controlled them all.
I knew exactly what I wanted for supper, and I
moved away from the reef to find it, propelling
myself along the bottom with long, smooth leg
strokes. A big cuda followed me, drifting alongside effortlessly. He was a five-footer, easy, and
mossy-colored with age. I didn't mind. If he
wanted the fish I shot, he was welcome to it. I
would just get another.

I was after a nice hogfish, and I finally saw one
beneath a sea fan in a clearing of coral sand. At
first he was pallid gray in color, but at my approach he flushed a bright nervous crimson, the
black spot at the base of the posterior ray vivid.
It was a beautiful fish, about a six-pounder, and I
took him cleanly with a shot through the head.
He fluttered briefly on the free shaft, then fell
still—and that's when I realized something other
than the barracuda had been following me.

Attracted by the death vibration—or the earlier
love vibrations—a huge open-water mako shark
came slashing across the reef, its massive pointed

head swinging back and forth as it vectored in on me and the dying hogfish.

Sharks and I are not exactly strangers. You won't meet a SEAL who hasn't had some kind of encounter with one. SEAL—sea, air and land commandos, the toughest of the tough and the roughest of the rough. And we just spend too much time in the water, day and night, to miss. For me, it was a night swim long, long ago on a training mission in the Pacific, one of those freak occurrences: a big dusky shark that wasn't supposed to be in those waters, and sure as hell wasn't supposed to attack. He left me with 148 stitches in my side and a new nickname. It was some scar. But strangely, Lee Johnson had come to be fascinated by it, paying it special, tender attention in our lovemaking. At any rate, I didn't want or need any more scars. I already had more than my share.

That mako was a beautiful creature: bright blue and then cobalt; a massive ten or eleven feet in length and probably weighing half a ton. The smaller species of shark don't bother me. They really don't. You learn to live with them. Besides, their instincts tell them to eat fish, not people. Believe me, if sharks ever got a taste for human flesh, there wouldn't be a saltwater beach on earth that was safe. But this mako was big enough to break all the rules.

The reef that had been alive with fish was suddenly still. They knew. This was more than just another big shark—this was a big shark feeding. He came toward me, his head slicing back and forth like a radar antenna. From the leg sheath, I drew my Randall attack-survival knife—the good-luck charm that had saved my life and had taken others more than once. But against this fish, it would be no more lethal than a bee sting. I drew it only as a prod. If it decided on me as supper, I could only try to jab its pointed snout and hope to scare it away.

I had been down a long time and was almost out of air. But I couldn't afford to try to surface. Sharks like dangling arms and legs. I thought about Lee back on the little Whaler, and I prayed that she wouldn't choose this moment to dive in and cool off. I watched the mako drawing closer and closer. He looked like a two-man mini-sub with fins and dead yellow eyes. I clung to a chunk of staghorn coral, and when he passed me the first time, I felt my legs drawing up behind me, swept along in his powerful wake. He had been close enough to take me in a bite.

But this mako, big as he was, had no interest in breaking the rules this day. He circled me once more, and still I hung motionless. Then, in one lightning swoop, he opened his brutish jumble of teeth, took up the hogfish, shook the spear free, then bolted back toward the reef, his head still jerking, his tiny brain still fixed on feeding. I didn't give him a moment to reconsider.

I surfaced on the side of the Whaler away from the reef and jumped into the boat with one kick of my Dacor TX-1000 Competition Class fins. Lee was in tears, still naked, but trembling.

"God, Dusky, I saw him coming . . . I kept screaming at you, but you never . . ."

She fell against me, crying.

As I started the Whaler and powered us back to my cruiser, Lee, wrapped in a blanket, leaned against me. I made jokes; I got her laughing. And I waited for the fear to catch up with me. That's the way it happens when you've had a close call—the fear doesn't come until later.

But it never arrived. Why? I wondered. And then I thought I knew: compared with the murders of my family and my best friend by the pirates, the drug runners—the ruthless ones who will forever operate in the Florida Keys—death in the grips of a creature so magnificent as that mako seemed rather pure and compelling.

My sleek charterboat was beautiful in that strange afternoon light. It is painted a deep night blue, with the words

Sniper
Key West, Florida

painted in small white script on the transom. It looked black against the soft blue of calm sea and against the backdrop of the island's sweeping white beach. We puttered up and I tethered the Whaler off on a long line, tossed out a small stern anchor, and then climbed aboard to receive the second shock of the day. We were not alone on the boat.

A gnomelike man stood on the deck. Gifford Remus. Old as he was, he looked at me with the same submissive uneasiness as always; the face of a little kid in the audience of some idolized big brother. And what he held in his gnarled hands brought all the saffron omens of sunset into sharp focus.

He smiled a wondrous smile, eyes wide, then held out a six-foot length of old Spanish chain.

It was made of pure gold.

2

I was so startled by his presence that my first reaction was anger.

"What the hell are you doing on this boat without my permission?"

The smile never even left his face. He kept looking at that chain of gold, fondling it as if it were a living thing. I doubt if he even heard me.

Gifford Remus—a comic and familiar figure on the streets of Key West. In age, he was anywhere from forty-five to sixty. He was a spindly little guy with a round head and a thatch of thin brown hair that you rarely saw beneath the soiled fishing cap he always wore. In town, he rode one of those old standard bicycles with thick tires, the chrome worn to patches on the handlebars. He was a scavenger. He picked up bottles and aluminum cans from alongside the road, stacking them neatly in the milk-crate basket that was bolted to the rear fender of the bike. He liked chrome doodads: horns and bells and colorful spinners that whirred in the wind as he pedaled down Duval Street in Old Town, smiling at the tourists and waving at the long-haired street bums who, I'm sure, felt their egos slightly elevated to see an individual more ragged-looking than themselves.

Gifford Remus. A simpleminded but likable man. He was smart enough—but strange. He seemed to exist in his own little world.

I had first seen him when I was barely a teenager. An orphan, I had been taken under the wing of a fine Italian family who made their living on the trapeze. Because I was so big, they had trained me early to be a catcher, and I loved it. I loved working high above the center ring, and I loved the circus, and I loved coming to Key West because my favorite writer—who had already become a legend on the island and around the world—would sometimes come to watch. Papa was fascinated by the big cats, and he seemed to enjoy watching us work the traps, too. I took to him, and he seemed to take to me. He gave me my first beer, and later, on what turned out to be one of his last visits to Key West, I watched him fork over a ten-dollar bill to a young islander who had asked only for spare change.

That islander was Gifford Remus.

When I finally gave up the SEALs, married, and started running a charterboat, Giff would occasionally approach me for a handout—that dull, toothless grin of his always in evidence, the strange little-boy eyes always blinking with thanks. Because I always gave. I remembered Papa, and I remembered what he had said that night.

"Let me tell you something, old-timer," he said. "There are only two things any of us really have to contribute to this world that's worth a damn. One thing's our honesty, and the other thing's our generosity. I'm not just talking about money. Real generosity goes far beyond money. But for an odd character like that guy, it takes the form of ten bucks."

Giff was an odd character, all right. He occasionally worked part-time jobs. But at heart he was a scavenger. And he scavenged more than just bottles and aluminum. With the little money he had, he kept an old wreck of a diesel inboard which he used to follow the big-time treasure hunters around. They hated him—but then, most treasure-hunter types hate just about everybody and everything except for themselves. Giff would anchor his old boat near their dig site and, when they were done for the day, dive down and look for the little scraps of coin or artifact they might have overlooked.

But there's no way anyone could have overlooked that chain.

"Giff! Hey—*Giff!*"

He stood on the deck as if he had been struck dumb. His old face was leather-brown from the sun, and it looked as if he hadn't shaved in a week. But his green eyes sparkled, as if the glint of the gold he held lasered straight through to his brain.

"Looka this, Dusky! Look here at what I . . ." He seemed to notice the presence of the woman for the first time, and he stopped in midsentence. Lee looked at me, both amused and perplexed.

"Lee, maybe you want to go below and change into something dry. It's my turn to cook tonight—right? I'll be down in a minute."

She pulled the blanket tight around her shoulders and hurried through the forward salon and down into the cabin.

I looked at Gifford Remus and his gold chain again, wiped my face with my hands, and gave him a seat in the port fighting chair.

"You want a beer, Giff?"

"Naw, Dusky. You know I don't drink."

I didn't know. I felt an odd sort of affection for him. I retrieved a cold Hatuey—that fine Cuban beer—from the salon locker, pulled on a T-shirt, and then sat beside him in the starboard chair. The beer was icy, and it sluiced the salt from my tongue. It was a pretty sunset: brilliant orange sphere melting into an oily sheen on the far turquoise horizon. Fish stirred in the shallows on Gull Keys, and pelicans soared in low formations, skimming the water.

"Let me see what you have there, Giff." He grinned crazily and handed me the chain. It was gold, all right. The weight of it surprised me. Draped vertically, it was almost as long as I am—and I'm six-two and a shade. It was made of hand-wrought links, each of them beautifully formed with spirals and smooth etching. The condition of it surprised me—it was such a lovely, unblemished yellow in color that it looked as if it might have just come from the jewelry store.

Giff seemed to be reading my thoughts. "It's gold, Dusky. Gold don't tarnish underwater. Had a few sandworms growin' around it, but I done knocked 'em off. Ain't it pretty?''

It was pretty indeed. I wondered about the Spaniard who had owned it—because it was certainly Spanish. For more than two hundred years they sailed along the Florida Straits to ravage the lands of Mexico and South America, enslaving and killing the Indians there as if they were little better than beasts of burden. What had he been like? Rich, certainly. A Spanish nobleman, perhaps. One of the aloof ones who loved gold and the Christian God: one of the many early ones who saw nothing wrong in building his fortune through the sweat and suffering of native Americans.

But on that last trip, he and his fellow Spaniards had been the ones to suffer. I took a cold sip of beer and studied the flat bronze sea which spread out before me. It was so peaceful, so deceptively deadly. I knew how it must have been. A shifting wind, and a massive sea churned to bile green with waves two stories high. Rain and relentless wind—and then the unseen reef. The reef from which Lee and I had just come? Perhaps. I pictured the terrified long-gone Spaniard praying for mercy after the galleon struck the reef, his words lost in the roar of sea and storm. But there had been no mercy. And now there was only ballast stone and, perhaps, a line of cannon somewhere beneath us in the coral sands to tell his story.

And this gold chain.

"Looks like you struck it rich, Giff."

The strange little man nodded with excitement. "Ain't it somethin', Dusky? An' I found it on my own, I did. I wasn't working no one else's site this time. You ever hear of the *Gaspar* fleet?"

I nodded my head. Treasure stories are a dime a dozen in Key West. In ten years, I had probably been approached a hundred times by men who wanted me to go hunt treasure with them. It was always a sure thing, and they always knew exactly where the galleon had gone down, and they always just needed a few more dollars to get them over the hump. And, in one way or another, the bulk of them ended up in ruin. Because of that, I rarely even took the time to listen to their offers. I just turned them down flat. But I had heard of the *Gaspar* fleet—who in Key West hadn't? It was said that the person who found the treasure section of the sunken *Gaspar* would be rich enough to buy anything—his own country, if he wanted. But I had never cared enough to learn the details, so I let Gifford Remus talk.

"Been studyin' about it all my life, Dusky. Put durn near every penny I had into researchin' it and keepin' up that old boat o' mine. I knew I'd find her; just *knew* this day would come." He chortled crazily. "For more than three hundred years folks has been lookin'—but it was me who found her."

I finished my beer and looked with sudden reappraisal at the man I had known only as a comic figure, a Key West scavenger. Was it possible that I—and everyone else—had mistaken his purity of purpose as just strangeness? Apparently. But could he have converted four decades of selling bottles and begging and hoarding a few odd gold coins into information that led him to the final resting spot of the *Gaspar*?

It didn't seem reasonable. But then nothing about treasure hunting is reasonable. Treasure hunting starts out as a hobby and becomes a disease. I had watched it ruin men, ruin their families, take the lives of their loved ones—yet still they pressed on. *Febris auris.* Gold fever. The bulk of them invest their lives and, if they're very, very lucky, get a few trinkets in return. And the little they find is enough to goad them on and on. I had met hundreds of treasure hunters, yet had never liked one of them. The two or three of them who were successful you had to admire for their intellect and their perseverance. But the bulk of them were like starstruck kids—completely engulfed in their own lives and their own dreams. And utterly ruthless. They cared only for themselves and the treasure which they were sure awaited them.

I didn't like seeing this new side of Gifford Remus.

It was nearly dusk now. Giff sat dreamily beside me, holding the chain in his lap, stroking it as if it were alive.

He said, "It was in 1622, Dusky. September. A whole fleet of Spanish ships—the Flota de Tierra Firme, they called it—sailed from Havana, bound for Spain. Those old wooden ships was loaded down heavy, Dusky—dyes and spices and rich noblemen. But mostly the cargo was gold, and silver from the Potosí mine in the Andes. Freshly minted, in coin and huge bars. The vice-flagship was the *Gaspar*. And she was some ship for those times. But no wooden boat was ever made to carry the durn load she was carryin'—almost two million dollars' worth of treasure. Worth probably six *hundred* million now. Can you imagine the weight of that? Six hundred million dollars in gold and silver!"

No, I couldn't. But I knew that Gifford Remus could. His eyes seemed to sparkle with the thought of it. He had imagined the weight and the color and the sight of it a thousand times over.

"So what happened, Giff?"

He snorted and picked at his nose. "Hurricane." He pointed toward the horizon off the stern of the *Sniper*. "Them ships got separated in the hurricane of 1622 right out there. Lord, I can almost *see* 'em. Overloaded, crashing into that blowin' sea. It was nighttime. An' the only sounding equipment they had was an ol' lead line, loaded with soap. The *Gaspar* foundered this way and struck the reef, then broke apart. Two more galleons went down that night and a couple more fleet tenders. Ain't no real secret what reef they hit, and folks has been lookin' for that treasure a long time. But I'm the only one to figure out why nobody's found the main lode. Even with all their fancy gear, I'm the only one to figure it out!" He motioned vaguely toward the huge expanse of water between the Marquesas where we were anchored and Fullmoon Cay. "It's all right out—"

"Hold it, Giff." I didn't like what he was leading up to. "Before you go any farther, I want you to tell me something. If you've worked all this time alone trying to find the *Gaspar*, why are you telling me about it? Why are you showing me the chain?"

He looked surprised. " 'Cause we're friends, Dusky!"

"Giff, that's true. But I still don't see—"

"You was the only one in Key West I could count on, Dusky! You was the only one who didn't laugh at me! Them other folks was wrong— I ain't crazy. I ain't no fool. Papa always knew. He knew what I was lookin' for an' he always give me money. And he give money to my ol' daddy when he was alive an' looking for the *Gaspar*. I thought you knew, too, Dusky. I thought we was sorta partners."

Partners.

I eyed the odd old man beside me. He swung back and forth in the fighting chair like a little kid on a drugstore stool. The wind was warm off the sea, and it carried with it the musky odor of the nearby islands, and the petroleum smell of Gifford's old boat, which he had tied and bumpered along the starboard side of the *Sniper*. What strange worlds exist in the narrow cranium space of the human mind. Because I had occasionally given him a few bucks and hadn't jeered at him, he considered me his partner.

"Giff, I appreciate that. I really do," I said. "But I want you to do yourself a favor. Don't tell me or anyone else where you found that chain. People have always gone a little crazy when they hear about someone finding gold—but especially now, when it's headed toward a thousand dollars an ounce. You tell the wrong person, Giff, and you could end up with a knife in your back."

He didn't even seem to hear me. With tiny hands, he pulled off his fishing cap and brushed back his thin hair. "You know what I'm gonna do with all my money, Dusky? I thought about this a lot. First, I'm gonna get me a new bicycle. A nice shiny one, and it's gonna be blue. A pretty blue. I'm gonna buy all sorts of horns and bells for it, and you know what else? A *radio* that clamps right onto the handlebars. Can you imagine?"

"If you sell that chain by weight alone, you could buy yourself a thousand bicycles, Giff."

He nodded quickly. "I know, I know. And there's a lot more than this chain down there, Dusky. I ain't found the rest of it yet, but it's there. It's the *Gaspar*. Big bars o' silver that weigh as much as eighty pounds, and piles an' piles of gold and silver coins. Pieces of eight, Dusky—just imagine!" The little man sat staring off to sea, caught up in and shocked by the new reality of his long-loved fantasy.

"Giff, I don't want to spoil anything for you, but have you considered that that chain might not have come from the *Gaspar*? You said yourself other ships went down in that hurricane. And over the years probably a dozen ships hit that reef and sunk. This is a treacherous area, Giff."

"Cabeza de los Mártires—that's what the Spaniards called it. Martyrs' Head. You're right, Dusky. A lot of ships went down here. They hated it. They were afraid of it." He made a sweeping motion with his arm. "Thousands o' people drowned right here. And they died screamin'; terrified. Next thing to hell, for them.

Deepwater shoaling into reefs and then a big point of shallow sand. It was an evil place in the minds o' them Spaniards. Evil an' haunted with all the dead. Fullmoon Cay over there is supposed to be alive with ghosts—get it? *Alive* with ghosts?" Gifford chuckled wildly at his own joke. "Still some folks won't go on it." He turned toward me, his eyes round and filled with strange emotion. "But you know somethin' else, Dusky? It's true. This place is haunted. That's how I found out where the treasure lode of the *Gaspar* ended up. I was camped out there on the beach on the Marquesas. And a ghost came to me one night. He was dressed in armor an' had a beard. Sounds crazy, I know—but it was the ghost of an old Spanish man. It weren't th' first time I talked to a ghost, Dusky. Spirits are thick all over Key West. Old pirates and sailin' men—they still roam the streets there, an' it's only me—old Gifford Remus, yes sir—they choose to talk to. It's because I got the vision, Dusky. It's because I got second sight—always have had it. Born with a veil over my face, I was. So I was layin' there asleep in my camp and I wasn't surprised a bit to wake up an' see that Spaniard standin' over me. He told me all about the *Gaspar*, Dusky. He was on it." Gifford held up the gold chain momentarily. "This necklace was *his*. Only part of the *Gaspar* sank when it hit the reef. That's why no one has ever found the treasure. In fact, those big rich treasure hunters wouldn't believe where it was if I tried to tell 'em. But the Spaniard knew, Dusky. And only you can help me get the rest of it. The Spaniard tol' me that, too. He said find you. Listen to this, Dusky—the treasure can be found right over . . ."

Gifford Remus turned to point, but at that moment Lee came out of the cabin.

"I hope you two men are hungry!"

I smiled at her. She was dressed in jeans and a blue denim shirt that was buttoned only halfway up. Her blond hair was tied into a thick ponytail with a bow, and she smelled pleasantly of the coconut oil I had rubbed her with earlier. The way Gifford suddenly clammed up told her that she had interrupted, and she was momentarily embarrassed. I reached over, took her leg and pulled her close, and made introductions. But Gifford wasn't interested in talking or staying for Lee's surprise supper. He stood up nervously, stammered out his thanks and climbed down into his boat. But before he left, he took me aside and forced the gold chain into my hand.

"Dusky, you got to keep this for me," he said. He spoke with a strange desperation that made me feel more than a little uneasy. "You got to hide it someplace. I'll be back in Key West in jus' a few days—give it back to me then."

"Giff," I said, "this is crazy. You shouldn't trust anyone—"

"The ghost tol' me, Dusky. They're followin' me, and—"

I shook him gently by his frail shoulders. "Come on, Gifford—who are 'they'?"

"You got to keep it for me until I get back, Dusky. I'll tell you everything then. We're both gonna be rich. We're partners, right? You an' me, Dusky—we're gonna salvage the *Gaspar* together.

An' then no one will ever laugh at ol' Gifford Remus again!''

He climbed nervously down into his old wreck of a boat, looking this way and that, filled with his strange visions and fears. And then puttered away into the darkness, back toward his camp on the nearby island.

3

It was a restless autumn night. The *Sniper* lifted
and rolled easily on her ground tackle, and a gentle wind drifted our way out of the tropics. A half
mile off the island, we rolled with the sea. A good
night for loving. A good night for sleeping. When
it's not too hot, and there are no bugs, there is no
place nicer than a boat at night. Above the massive vee-berth forward, there is a screened hatch
that is wide enough for even someone my size to
crawl through. But after Lee and I had finished
our loving, I wanted to do nothing but lie there
and look up through the hatch at the star mist
which began to rise and roll as if it were a sea in
the sky.

I was soon asleep. A light restless sleep filled
with wispy dreams. Gifford Remus introduced me
to his ghost. The ghost wore the golden chain
which, earlier, I had stashed within the forward
bilge, far off to one side.

"How do you do, Captain MacMorgan?"

"Very well, sir. I've heard so much about you, sir."

Sir?

"Captain, I want you to know why you have been the one chosen to salvage the treasure from my long-lost *Gaspar* . . . *Gaspar* . . . *Gaspar* . . ."

Restless dreams on a restless night; dreams that soon became nightmares . . .

Explosions in rain forests, and the pleas of friends. Midnight-colored rivers and the shock of being taken from behind. Broken cars and broken loved ones, and then I was being pulled down, down, down. . . .

I sat bolt upright in the vee-berth. Something was wrong. I rubbed my face and realized that I was sweating. Lee was gone. That I knew. Earlier, after we had made love until we could love no more, I had heard her tiptoe from the bed and had watched her pull a T-shirt over her lithe nakedness. Sometimes you just want to be alone.

And then I knew. *Sniper* wasn't riding right at anchor. When you know a boat well, you can feel the slightest change in trim and motion, and every change can be a danger signal. We seemed to be sliding sideways. As if we were being pulled. And just as I realized it, that's when I heard the scream and the splash.

I jumped naked from the bed and ran aft in the darkness. I miscalculated the steps and gave my left shin a painful crack on some invisible corner.

"*Shit!*"

I could still hear splashing, and I heard Lee calling my name in desperation. She seemed to be getting farther and farther away. I hit the toggle switch and the deck lights flashed on. The deck was empty. The girl was gone; she was somewhere on or in the dark sea.

"Lee!"

I heard her voice again. Off the stern. And more thrashing. And just as I crouched to dive in after her, I heard, "No, Dusky—don't! There's something in here! Don't!"

My mind, still gauzy with sleep, struggled to figure out just what in the hell was going on. And then I knew. Every evening of the trip, I had baited a grouper hook, stripped off line, and then anchored the big Penn International reel in a stern rod holder. The big boat rod was bending now, playing out line as if we had hooked a submarine. That's what had altered the motion of the *Sniper*; that's what was pulling us sideways. Some huge fish. And somehow, Lee had gotten tangled in the line and been pulled overboard.

I forced myself to be calm; to think.

"*Dusky . . . awwww . . .*"

In one swift motion, I grabbed the assault rifle which I kept in spring clips over the main controls and headed up the ladder to the flybridge. My hands trembled as I jerked the chrome 500,000-candlepower searchlight around. The white shaft of light tunneled through the darkness, exposing a light mist that oozed off the glassy water. I scanned back and forth, back and forth—and then I saw her. About fifty yards out, but still moving, being pulled by something. She looked pathetically small in that harsh light. Her blond hair was matted over her face as she struggled to free herself.

And then, suddenly, she was free. She submerged for a moment as the woven eighty-pound-test line went slack, then came back up calling to me, "It's okay, Dusky! I'm loose now! Hey, Dusky! I made it!"

She was loose, all right. But she hadn't made it. Not yet. With the searchlight, I scanned the water behind her. And finally I saw what I had prayed would not be there—the huge mako shark I had encountered earlier that day. It was about a hundred yards off, just a few degrees port of stern, and it was closing in on Lee.

The shark was right at the edge of visibility, its triangular dorsal fin looking a ghostly gray in the shaft of light. It was now circling Lee, getting closer and closer.

"Lee! Stop swimming . . . *Lee!*"

But still she splashed on with strong, choppy strokes. She was headed for the Whaler, which was anchored off the stern. But she wasn't going to make it. Suddenly, the huge mako began to angle toward her. This was his sea, his feeding time. To the shark, this new woman in my life was just a big fish struggling in the darkness, something to swallow so that he might continue his life of instinct and death.

I switched the assault rifle from semiautomatic to automatic. It was some weapon—a Russian AK-47. I had smuggled it back from Nam in the tripod case some of the journalists over there carried. It had a sighting range of eight-hundred meters, and was capable of firing ninety rounds a minute. But I had only a thirty-round clip, and I had to make sure I got at least fifteen or twenty of those rounds into the head of that shark.

I braced my left arm on the searchlight so I could move it on the trail of the shark as I fired. The metal butt plate was cold against my bare shoulder. I leveled it, fixed the peep sight about three feet forward of the dorsal fin, began to exhale slowly, then squeezed the trigger.

Pop-pop-pop-pop-pop . . .

The first burst was too high and a little to the left. The tip of the shark's gray-black dorsal exploded off its back. But still the mako kept getting closer to Lee, vectoring in on the splashes of her weakening crawl stroke.

My hands were shaking. This one had to be it. The shark was only twenty-five yards from her and closing fast. I took another deep breath and opened up.

Pop-pop-pop-poppa-thud-thud-thud.

I was on him now, and I held the trigger down, hearing the sweet sound of slugs smacking into solid flesh. The huge mako breached, then jumped. His yellow eyes caught the light and he seemed to be staring right at me.

You should have gotten me earlier, buster. You had your chance . . .

And then he thrashed away, belly up, in a wild and final death frenzy.

I ran back down to the deck and climbed over onto the boarding platform. Lee pulled herself along the Whaler, and then I lifted her out. She was dripping and trembling with cold. The T-shirt was plastered against her chest, transparent in the deck lights.

She stood up shakily. "Thanks, pal. There was either one big fish out there, or a small airplane crashed behind me."

"You guessed it, woman. A small plane. Shot it down just in time. Let's get you dried off."

I started the gas stove while Lee toweled off. I made tea, strong, and added a healthy dollop of brandy in each mug. We sat in the little galley booth facing each other. She had pulled on a pair of jeans and my black Navy watch sweater. Her cheeks were flushed with cold and her eyes sparkled a deepwater blue. I had never seen her look prettier. That's what a close call does to you. It's the hallmark of a brush with death. It heightens your senses and sweeps the fog of drudgery from your eyes. And as much as I hated admitting it to myself, I loved it. In my happy, happy years of marriage, I had forgotten how much. But once you have walked the razor's edge, once you have put everything on the line and the only thing between you and death is the squeeze of a trigger or the arch of a knife, you can never ever stop loving it. And in that moment I knew what the future held for me. I knew that I could never give it up again.

"Feeling a little better?"

She made a funny face. "Absolutely. Say, what's in this brandy, anyway?"

"I think they call it alcohol."

"Hum . . . I think it might catch on. Be a big seller with ladies who almost get eaten by sharks." She reached over with a small tanned hand and stroked my face. "Thanks, Dusky."

I winked at her. "Anytime, pal. But why don't you tell me how you happened to be going for a swim at"—I checked my Rolex briefly—"three A.M.?"

She forgot her close call and began to laugh. "Clumsiness, Captain. I hate to admit this, but you have been squiring around one of the all-time clumsy ladies. After our . . . after the last time we made love, I went out to get some air. I wanted to think, Dusky. So much has happened in the last month, I just wanted to be alone and sort it out. . . ."

It was a subject we had been skirting for the last week or so. I knew it had been on her mind, and I suspected what her decision was. But the topic upset her. It took the color from her cheeks and averted her eyes. I didn't want to hear it. Not now.

"You were telling me how you happened to be in the water, woman."

"Oh! Well, when I was walking on the deck, I noticed that there was something on your grouper line. So I started reeling it in. It was some kind of pretty yellow-colored snapper, Dusky. A great big one. I got him to the surface, reached over, and wrapped the line in my hand—and the next thing I knew I was in the water!"

She had had a close call, all right. The mako had come up and taken the fish at the surface. And she had gotten tangled in the line. Had the mako sounded, she would have drowned. And if I hadn't had the assault rifle, she would have died an even nastier kind of death.

"Do you think my scar would have been as

pretty as yours, Dusky?" There was a gentleness
in the way she flirted now. That almost tangible
look of passion was gone, replaced by something
that was even more valuable and desirable.

"Everything about you is prettier than me, Lee.
Everything."

She lifted my hand and kissed it gently.
"Dusky, this last month has been so very, very
fine. I can't tell you how much . . ."

I looked deep into her eyes. "Then don't,
woman." I stood up and switched on the little
Sony transistor radio. I toyed with the dial until I
got something moody but not too sweet. Perfect
music for the parting scene. Like in a movie. But
my unhappiness was tempered by the knowledge
that it could be no other way. She stood up and
pulled me to her, rubbing her hands across my
bare chest.

"You know, don't you, Dusky?"

"Yes," I said. "Yes, I know."

I felt her start to tremble a little, on the verge
of tears. "Dusky, I just can't go away and leave
him like that. He deserves another chance. My
husband was good once, Dusky. Like you. Good
and brave and strong. What is it about the world
that wrecks people? Does the business world rob
all people of their souls?"

"Some," I lied. "But he can get it back. You two
can work it out, Lee. I just hope he knows how
lucky he is. Strong women aren't all that easy to
come by."

A touch became a caress, and a look became a
kiss, and with a solemn, sad light in her eyes she
stripped her clothes off, letting me enjoy the sight

of her, because we both knew that this would be the last time. We made long, slow love then; a giving kind of love, making affectionate presents of ourselves. And finally, after a long time, we let our emotion join and peak in a great bursting swell. And then we drifted off to sleep; Lee still atop me, still intertwined as if we couldn't bear to let it end.

And the next day, we were strangers once again. Polite, smiling, and infinitely cordial—but strangers all the same. The emotional dynamics of the human being are beyond understanding sometimes. In just a few hours, in the space of one decision, we had transformed ourselves from the most intimate lovers to a friendly man and a friendly woman who just happened to be sharing the same bed, the same boat. I could expect nothing else from a woman of Lee's character—indeed, she would have disappointed me had she acted otherwise. Before, she had been separated from her husband both physically and emotionally. But now, with her decision to return, to give it one more chance, she had reacknowledged her long-ago vows, and infidelity just wasn't in that woman's makeup. It seemed so absurd but, at the same time, so reasonable—ever admirable.

What crazy little games we all play.

As always, I was up at first light. A beautiful dawn. I sat on the flybridge and watched the sun spreading over the eastern horizon, changing the earth. It was a good morning to break rules. So I got myself a cold Hatuey from the beer locker and sat on the flybridge in the fresh heat of morning.

No human being should be allowed to die without watching sunrise at sea. The islands of the Marquesas came into slow focus, transformed from black to soft gray, to green. Palm trees and Australian pines, leaning in windward strands, caught the light at angles, seeming to stand out, set apart, from the white sweep of beach. The sea was oiled and black, then black-blue, and cumulus clouds on the western horizon glowed with the golden cragginess of the Colorado mesas. White wading birds left their roosts on Mooney Harbor Key and flew in formation toward the sun and burst into flames.

By the time Lee got up, I had eggs and fish frying. She gave me a sisterly kiss, suddenly bashful, then sat in the galley booth while I served her and pressed awkward jokes.

"What are you reading?"

She held up the book. "*Far Tortuga* by Peter Matthiessen. I found it in your library locker."

"How do you like it?"

"You were right, Dusky—it's one of the most beautiful books I've ever read."

So we made small talk and small jokes, and avoided touching one another with hands or with eyes. And while I got *Sniper* ready for the trip back to Key West, she sat in her bikini on the foredeck, taking in the sun and reading.

I wanted to see Gifford Remus once more before heading back. His actions the day before hadn't seemed exactly normal, and I wanted to make sure he was all right. I started the twin 453 GMC diesels, enjoying the sweet muffled roar they made, shoved her into gear, then nosed ahead

through the clear shallows. From my vantage
point on the flybridge, I saw a huge ray fly away
from us at an angle, and coral heads stood apart
from the white sand, alive with grouper and
snapper—all magnified in size by the water.

The shallows off the Marquesas and Fullmoon
Cay are trickey areas. You don't want to mess
with them at night. It has nothing to do with the
natural hazards which had sunk the *Gaspar* and
ships like it. These hazards are man made; the
result of years of serving as a target area for the
planes from the Navy base at Key West. The best
known target wreck is the Navy destroyer *Patricia*,
but there are plenty of others, too—all the victims
of U.S. bombs and high-caliber slugs. So I took it
easy. We had a good coming tide, and I nosed
Sniper right up into the shallows of the long
white beach of the Marquesas where I expected
Giff to be.

But he wasn't there. His ragged canvas tent was
still pitched, flapping in the soft breeze, and his
campfire still smoldered.

"I'm going to go ashore and have a look
around," I told Lee.

She smiled at me and winked. "And have a
dip?"

It had become a standing joke with us. I never
smoke, but I enjoy an occasional pinch of snuff.
It's something I learned to love as a kid; a habit I
had converted into a weapon over in Nam. An
adversary is in too much pain to fight when he
has Copenhagen in his eye. But no matter how
much I loved it, I was aware that some ladies
aren't exactly enamored with the idea of their suit-

ors taking a chaw of tobacco. But Lee didn't mind. And it amused her that I only dipped when she wasn't around.

"Yeah," I said. "And have a dip."

I had hoped that Giff's boat was anchored on the other side of the island, in Mooney Harbor. But it wasn't. I pushed my way back through the mangroves, dodging the clumps of sandspurs. I wore only khaki shorts, and the mosquitoes feasted on my bare legs. I pushed back the flaps of his tent and looked inside. His sleeping bag was in a heap, and beside it there were two plastic garbage bags. I opened the first one. Aluminum beer cans and Coke bottles.

The scavenger. Ever the scavenger.

But I was surprised at what was in the other sack. It was heavy, and when I opened it I could smell the foul salt odor of sea rack. I stuck in my hand and pulled out a piece of pottery. It was very old, covered with moss and tunicates. Spanish? I studied the intricate design on the lip of what must have been an old wine vase. Yes, probably Spanish. The garbage bag was half full of pottery scraps and some kind of black goo, a viscous substance that smelled vaguely of pine pitch. And just as I was about to drop it back into the sack, I noticed something. A flash of silver; a bright glimmer from within the goo. I cleaned it off enough for me to see. It was an oddly shaped coin. There was a cross on it and, within each right angle formed by the cross, there were lionlike crests. I pulled more of the goo away and found more coins—a hundred or more, all encased and preserved in the goo. Gifford Remus had struck it rich, all right. It might not have been the mother lode, and it might or might not have been the *Gaspar*. But he had found his treasure, treasure aplenty to buy the new bicycle he had dreamed of.

I waded back out to the *Sniper* and scanned the open water with my Bushnell-made zoom scope. The shallows off the Marquesas look so small on the chart, but seem so endless when you are on them. No wonder no one had yet found the *Gaspar*—or the dozens of other galleons and ships that rested beneath the sands there. And it didn't really surprise me that Gifford was not to be seen. He was in a small, small boat on one huge stretch of water. His treasure site was probably nowhere near the Marquesas. He was someplace out there, on the blue sheen of sea. And I could picture him diving and hunting, those wide old eyes of his searching crazily for the gold he had always dreamed of finding.

I remembered what one of the circus's ten-in-one-show magicians had told me once: *The only thing worse than having no dreams is to realize your dreams.* And I wondered what Gifford Remus would do now that his lifetime search was over.

"Do you see him?" Lee stood behind me, scanning the distance.

"No, but I'm sure he's okay. Just a little crazy. I'll give him his chain when he gets back to Key West."

She reached up and put her hand on my shoulder. "He trusts you, Dusky. Everybody trusts you. He made a wise choice. I hope my decision is just as wise. . . ."

4

It was a small item in the Key West *Citizen*. A short news story with a small headline: "Local Man Missing, Boat Found Adrift."

It was Hervey Yarbrough who brought it to my attention. I had stopped by his ramshackle house and marina on Cow Key to buy some brass wood screws. Hervey is a chunky, pug-nosed guy with a beard, one of the few native Key Westers still around. Most of them have been driven out by the influx of tourists and drug runners, and the decline of fishing. But Hervey had kept ahold of his jungled acreage on the bay, refusing persistent offers from developers which promised him eternal wealth if he would only allow them to come in and bulldoze his land flat and build the anonymous and sterile concrete condominium grotesqueries which now plague Florida.

"Not no—but *hell* no!" Hervey always told them.

So I walked down the dirt drive and found Hervey hard at work scraping the bottom of a boat.

Slaughtered barnacles lay in heaps beneath the boat, and flies buzzed over them merrily.

"Well, well, looka what the cat's done drug in!" he greeted me, smiling broadly. "Hope you know that daughter o' mine is jes' jealous as can be at you goin' off with that blond woman from New York."

I grinned, shook my head, and said nothing. You learn to expect such things from islanders. I had told no one about the trip Lee and I had taken, yet he knew. And his beautiful eighteen-year-old daughter, April, knew. And his wife, I was sure, knew too. God only knows how the islanders find out all the stuff they do. But when you want world news, you pick up a paper. When you want to find out what's going on in Key West, you ask an islander.

"Need some wood screws, Hervey. Brass. One of my forward railings is starting to work loose and I want to fix it before it starts to score the planking."

He took a couple more long swipes at the barnacles, wiped his hands on his pants, and put down the scraper.

"Heard you were out off the Marquesas, Dusky."

I followed him up the path toward the wooden shed he had converted into part store, part warehouse. "Yeah. Nice weather. Got into some late dolphin, and saw one hell of a big mako. Thousand pounds, I'd say."

"No kiddin'?" He pushed open the door of the shed and flicked on the bare overhead bulb. The shed smelled of dank wood and marine hardware.

"Thousand pounds, huh?" He began to rummage around through assorted boxes, looking for the screws I wanted, all the while telling me a shark story of his own. In other small towns, local residents use weather as the bottom-line topic of conversation. In Key West, they use sharks. "In fact," he finished, "I was tellin' the old lady last night that it was probably a shark tha' got ol' Gifford Remus."

He suddenly had my attention. "What?"

"Gifford Remus—you know him. That weird little ol' guy who's always riding around on that bicycle—"

"I know who he is—but what makes you think a shark got him?"

Hervey reached over, grabbed the *Citizen* from the desk, and flipped through it. "This is what makes me think that. You mean you ain't heard?"

The story read:

Coast Guard officials in Key West reported they discovered a 22-foot diesel skiff adrift off Fullmoon Cay yesterday. An early investigation indicates that the vessel belongs to Gifford Remus, age 51, of 935 Banyan Street.

A Sheriff's Department spokesman said that eyewitnesses reported that Remus left Garrison Bight Harbor nearly two weeks ago in this boat. His destination was not ascertained. When Coast Guard authorities discovered the boat, there was hull damage and it was partially submerged.

Remus was a familiar figure on the streets of Key West. A native, Remus rode the

streets on a bicycle and made his living selling aluminum cans and soft-drink bottles. He
was known to give pennies to babies, and
Key West children often called him "Uncle
Giff."

The Coast Guard is presently fronting an
air-sea search of the Marquesas area. Boaters
and commercial fishermen who have any information regarding Remus are asked to contact the Monroe County Sheriff's Department
or Coast Guard authorities.

I put the paper down. So Giff was officially
missing. Not necessarily dead—but what else
could have separated him from his skiff? Hervey
saw the concern on my face.

"Hey—you knowed that ol' man, didn't you?"

"Like I know most of the stray dogs in this
town. I gave him a few bucks, and he mated for
me every now and then. I'm a soft touch, Hervey.
And I might be the last person to have seen him—
out off the Marquesas."

"Hey, you better tell the law about that, huh?"

I took another look at the newspaper story. "I
plan to, Hervey. Did you know that Remus was
a treasure hunter?"

Hervey paused, thinking for a moment, tugging
at his black beard. "Well, now that you mention
it, I guess I did hear somethin' about that. But
heck, Dusky, everybody's a treasure hunter
around here 'cept you an' me—and I ain't too sure
about me sometimes." He laughed.

"What exactly did you hear about Remus?"

Hervey reached into his back pocket and pulled

out a fresh packet of Red Man chewing tobacco. He opened it reflectively, jammed a massive chaw into his mouth, and spit. "Let me see here. This story goes way back. We both grew up here on the island, you know, and my daddy knew his daddy. You look at ol' Giff, and you figure he had to have a pretty weird upbringin'—but that ain't the way it was. His daddy was a fine man. Didn't look nothin' like Giff—which made a lot of the meaymouth people in this town talk, it did. His daddy looked a lot like you, matter o' fact. Big muscular guy with saltwater-blond hair. Always smilin'. Well, like the rest of the folks round here in the Keys, he fished and trapped turtle and ran a little rum when the money got tight. Now *he* was a treasure hunter. Giff's mama was from down in the islands; some kinda Spanish blood in her, 'cause she had crow-black hair an' the darkest eyes you ever seen. And it was her that filled Giff's daddy's head with all them stories about sunken' treasure. He was after one wreck in particular . . ."

"The *Gaspar*?"

"Yeah—that was it! Do you know this story?"

"I'll tell you what I know later. What about Giff's father?"

"Well, like I said, Giff's mama was always fillin' his head with these treasure stories. Don't know where she got 'em. Stories musta been passed down to her or somethin'. Now, she was a weird one, she was. Used to tell fortunes and stuff like that. Some folks said she was a voodoo woman or somethin'. I was about five years younger than Giff, but I still remember what happened. Fire.

They said one o' them candles she used to burn
fell over an' hit the curtains. She never made it
out of the house. God knows how Giff did—he
weren't but eleven or twelve. His daddy was off
someplace huntin' that treasure, and they both
went a little crazy after that. One night his daddy
came into Sloppy Joe's bar kinda wild-eyed, flash-
in' gold Spanish coins around. Said he'd found
the wreck he'd been lookin' for, and that he and
his son was rich. No one heard from him after
that. Key West has never had no shortage of rough
characters, an' folks figured he opened his mouth
to the wrong men. Didn't hear nothin' about Giff
bein' a treasure hunter till long afterwards. He'd
gotten crazier an' crazier, and it sorta surprised
me. Someone said to me, 'Hey, you know ol' Gifford Remus is still huntin' for that treasure his
daddy hunted for?' I thought that he'da had
enough of treasure huntin'. I admit I'm a supersti-
tious kinda guy, Dusky—name someone who
works around boats and the sea that ain't. But I'm
tellin' you, treasure huntin' is bad luck. All the
way around. I don't believe in ghosts and duppies
and such—not when it's daylight, anyway. But
you start huntin' for that old Spanish gold, and
you're just lookin' for trouble."

Hervey stopped and spit on the sand floor of
the wooden marina office. He grinned suddenly.
"Bet you think I'm crazy now—talkin' about
spooks and such."

"Absolutely. Now you can listen to me and decide how crazy I am."

So I told him about Gifford's sudden appearance on my boat. And about the gold chain, and

the silver coins at his camp. I even mentioned Gifford's Spanish ghost.

"So Giff wanted you to be his partner, huh?" Hervey tugged at his beard, thinking.

"Yeah. It didn't make any sense to me either. He was an old street friend and I gave him a few bucks now and then when he asked for it, but he'd never mentioned treasure hunting to me. In fact, I can't remember us talking about anything but the weather and his bicycle."

Hervey moved his chew from side to side with his tongue. "Well, like I said, you do kinda favor his daddy. Ol' Giff was odd enough that that might make a difference."

"So do you still think it was a shark that got him?"

"Well, I doubt if we'll ever know. Like that mako you run into—there's some awful big sharks out there an' he was by hisself, in an awful small boat. Coulda knocked a hole in the bottom an' ate him when ol' Giff fell out. Or it coulda been some other treasure hunters that got him. There's plenty workin' that area. Or it could be that Giff's out there on an island right now just waitin' to be rescued."

Hervey put a dozen brass wood screws in a paper sack and handed them to me. He switched off the overhead light and we walked back outside into the warm October day.

"Hervey," I said, "tell your wife and your daughter that I said hello—"

"Oh no you don't!" He grinned at me bawdily. "You ain't gettin' away without talkin' to April your own self. She ain't here right now—she's got a job waitin' tables up to Becker's Restaurant.

Savin' money so she can start college in January.
But I ain't passin' no messages between you two.
So come to dinner. Friday night?"

"When did you become a matchmaker?"

"Hah! I jus' want to see that muleheaded girl
o' mine light into you, that's all."

I smacked Hervey on the shoulder. He was a
good man, the descendant of sailing captains. Beneath his jovial exterior he was as tough and intelligent as they come.

"Okay," I said. "Friday night. What should I
bring?"

"A first-aid kit—that's about all you'll need!"

He was still heaving with laughter when I
walked up the dirt road, back toward Key West.

Detective Rigaberto Herrera wasn't in his office
when I arrived at the sheriff's office. A pleasant,
matronly-looking receptionist dutifully logged my
arrival and took a message for Rigaberto. He was
one of the thousands of Cubans who had escaped
Castro's takeover of that beautiful island country
ninety miles to the south and arrived in America
totally committed to building a new and respect-
able life for himself. Rigaberto had worked nights
to put himself through college, all the while studying and finally mastering the English language.
He asked for no favors and accepted none, and
had worked his way up steadily to the position
of detective. He was a very good man, and I
counted him as one of my best friends. I wanted
to find out what he knew about Gifford Remus.

"May I ask who's inquiring?" the woman at the
desk asked.

I told her my name, and I watched her face change.

"Captain MacMorgan," she said, "I was very, very sorry to hear about your wife and your sons. I met her only once, but I liked her immediately." She smiled momentarily. "She had . . . *class*."

I thanked her and meant it. The fine ones leave a trail in their passage through life; a legacy of honesty, lasting friendships, and strong ideals to the people around them and to the general human pool.

The matronly receptionist was right. My wife had had class. On my last day on the boat with Lee, I could not keep my thoughts from the woman I had lost. Was I wrong to look to another for comfort so quickly? No, no, certainly not. It can never be wrong to exchange warmth and affection in the universal void. Yet, as Lee and I parted, the words she spoke for the first time jarred my long-ignored base of Protestant morality, and I could not reply.

"*Dusky . . . I want you to know that . . . that I love you, love you so, and I will never forget you . . .*"

So the words I wanted to voice were left unspoken; my role left unplayed. I had hugged her quickly and turned from her tearful exit, and did not look back. Love was an indulgence I could no longer afford. It was a question of the future, and my future no longer included a wife, a family, harbors on cold nights. I was now a freelance, a troubleshooter. It had turned out that the men who had murdered my loves were also being pursued by a federal agency. The federal agency wanted someone local, someone tough, someone

with a military background, to walk the point for
them. I was a natural. For them, my first mission
was one of expedience. There was a Senator on a
private island who maintained his own little army
of drug runners. And they were making him
rich—until I came along. For me, it was a mission
of revenge. I was told to just shake them up; get
them nervous enough to make mistakes so that
when the federal boys came in with their warrants
the next day, there would be evidence aplenty.

Well, I shook them up all right. I went through
those burned-out drugheads like a machete
through a pumpkin. And with the evidence they
wanted, the federal boys also found more than a
few corpses.

I had made them pay. But not nearly enough.

I wanted another mission. Under the auspices of
the United States government, I wanted to loose myself once more on the pirates that always have and
always will feed off the weak in the Florida Keys.

And that's what I was thinking about as I
walked the streets of Key West on that fine October day. October is one of the best months in Florida. The weather is clear and warm, and most of
the tourists have gone home or haven't arrived.
Seas are calm, fishing good, and the rainy season
has just ended. At my marina, the charterboats
and pleasure yachts were lined across the basin in
orderly white formation, and there were some
kids fishing for snapper off the dock. A slow October day. Just the way I like it.

I went into the marina office to check my sched-
ule and to say my hellos and announce my return.
Stevie Wise, who lives on a houseboat and works

behind the cash register when he is not regaling a pretty tourist, was the only one around. Stevie is a popular guy around the docks—especially with the other live-aboards. For the married men, he's the epitome of their dreams of bachelorhood. He had left some dreary teaching job in Ohio to follow the free and easy life. He had purchased a clunker houseboat and grown a mustache. People say he looks a little like Paul McCartney, the singer. He flirts with wives, but does not touch. He throws cheap but enthusiastic parties and seems to get along with everyone. At spring break there always seemed to be between four and a dozen pretty northern coeds sleeping, dancing, or sunbathing on his floating home. And at the height of the tourist season, the wealthy kept beauties seemed to find his abode—which he'd named *Fred Astaire* for no good reason that I know of—both quaint and entertaining.

Stevie Wise seemed to be one happy guy.

But on this day he wasn't looking particularly happy. He sat on a folding chair looking bored and miserable. This slow time of year was obviously driving him crazy.

"Looks like I could have been busy—if I'd been around. How many of my cancellations rebooked with Captain Nels?"

"Fourteen or fifteen, I guess. He told me to thank you."

"Fishing been any good?"

"Sure, sure. It's always rotten for the tourists and always great if they charter a boat."

"We earn our money, we do."

Stevie put down the magazine he had been

reading. "Dusky, do you realize there hasn't been a pretty woman down here on the docks since you came back more than a week ago?"

"You poor devil," I said.

"Hey, I'm going to have a party Saturday night—invite everybody in town and see what turns up." He hesitated for a moment, unsure whether or not to invite me. And he asked, finally, "Want to come?"

"Maybe, Stevie. I just might."

The *Sniper* stood out dark blue among the white formation of charterboats. I stopped on the dock and straightened my sign:

CAPTAIN DUSKY MACMORGAN
BILLFISH, DOLPHIN, SHARKS, GROUPER
FULL DAYS, HALF DAYS—INQUIRE AT MARINA

Chartering isn't a bad business if you don't mind not making much money and putting up with an occasional asshole. It demands long days in the hot sun, acting pleasant when you feel anything but pleasant, and learning to control your temper when a party misses fish after fish because of inexperience, and then tries to blame you for a day that ends with nothing in the fishbox.

But that rarely happens. Most of the people you take out are friendly and anxious to learn, and often end up becoming friends. Chartering is less a business than it is a way of life, and I'll never give it up.

So I straightened my sign. I planned to spend an hour or two securing that loose forward railing, then take a shower up at the marina. The afternoon was reserved for cold beer and a good book.

But as I started to board, I noticed there was something different about my boat. It took me a moment to figure it out. The cabin door was ajar. And it had been locked when I left that morning.

I don't like surprises.

I took my folding Gerber knife from the sheath on my belt and stepped carefully onto the deck. I knelt by the door and listened. Voices. Two men. Nice people don't board a boat without an invitation. And they don't pick the locks of cabin doors. I know how to deal with people who aren't nice. They taught me in the SEALs and gave me on-the-job experience in Nam.

5

In one swift motion, I jerked open the cabin door and swung down into the galley, landing in a crouch, my knife poised and ready.

I had planned on taking them by surprise. I had planned on setting them down and making them tell me exactly what they were doing on my boat without my permission.

But sometimes things don't work out as you've planned. When I swung into the darkened cabin, my eyes finally adjusted enough for me to realize that I was looking down the stubby barrel of a .38 caliber Police Special.

"What the hell?"

"Dusky!"

And then we were all laughing; laughing, pointing at each other, and laughing some more. My two visitors turned out to be two friends. Rigaberto, my Cuban friend from the Sheriff's Department, and Norm Fizer, my connection with the federal agency, and a friend from long, long ago;

a guy I had worked with and learned to trust on one hush-hush mission in Cambodia.

"I must say, you know how to make an entrance, MacMorgan," Fizer said, still holding the pistol.

"I practice whenever someone breaks into my boat. What the hell are you two up to?"

Rigaberto not only looked confused, he looked resigned to his confusion. "Let him talk first," he said. "I'm still mixed up."

Norm Fizer chuckled. He has an easy laugh, one that complements his all-American-boy countenance. He looks like Jack Armstrong come of age. He has short dark hair, thick and well styled, and a wide rack of shoulders that the obligatory three-piece suit does a poor job of hiding. Everything is right out of Norman Rockwell: square jaw, wide, friendly eyes. And his diction tells you he went a lot farther than high school. He looks very proper, very businesslike—but I knew the other side of him. I had worked with him in Asia and I knew that he was as tough as he was dependable. In fact, I still can't figure out who in that bureaucratic wasteland called Washington, D.C., had the good sense to hire him.

"Your friend Rigaberto and I were just sitting here getting acquainted," Fizer chuckled.

"I tried to arrest him," Rigaberto said flatly. "I saw him prowling around your boat."

"And I thought he was one of the drug runners who got away and had come back to take one last shot at you."

I started laughing again. I couldn't help it. I

could picture those two stalking each other—
something right out of Abbott and Costello. "Well,
it looks like I'm the only one not on duty here, so
I think I'll have a beer. Anybody interested?"

They weren't. The good ones don't drink on the
job. And they were two good ones. I sat back
down at the little galley booth. "So," I said, "are
you two friends now? No scars? No hurt
feelings?"

Norm Fizer pressed a careful hand against his
ribs. "I think I'm okay—but I think I'll have some
X-rays taken just for my own peace of mind." He
winked at Rigaberto. "If you ever get tired of Key
West, I'm sure we could find a place in Washington for a guy who can handle himself the way
you do. God, what a punch!"

Rigaberto rubbed a spot on his cheek that was
already starting to swell. "You federal guys ought
to wear badges or something. I'm telling you,
there ought to be a law!"

Fizer cleared his throat, done with joking now.
"Dusky, Detective Herrera wants to talk with
you—is that right?"

Rigaberto nodded. "But it's nothing you can't
sit in on. From the credentials you showed me,
I'd say you've been cleared to sit in on anything
and everything—right up to the White House."

Norm gave one of his rare shy smiles. "Let's
just say that you can trust me."

Rigaberto turned to me. He's a rugged little guy
with classic Hispanic features: dark eyes, dust-
colored complexion, and a squatty, muscular
build. "Well, what I stopped down here for,

Dusky, is that I heard you'd been doing some cruising around the Marquesas."

"That seems to be one of the worst-kept secrets of my life."

"Key West is a small island, *amigo*," he said, flushing a little. "Anyway, I was just wondering if you happened to come across a guy named Gifford Remus—that odd little guy you always see—"

"Sure I know him, Rigaberto. I read in the paper today that he had disappeared, and I went by your office to tell you about it. I not only saw him, I talked with him. And it might have been the night before his boat went down."

Rigaberto took a pen and pad from his coat pocket and began to make notes. So I told him the whole story, everything. And I noticed how Norm's attention slowly homed in.

"Why did he think someone was following him? Do you know?" Rigaberto asked.

I shook my head. "Like you said, he was an odd little guy. Apparently he believed some Spanish ghost was trying to help him locate the treasure. The way he talked, the ghost had warned him."

Rigaberto grimaced. "Ghost, huh? Now I've heard everything. And some of you gringos think we Cubans are crazy."

I got up, went forward, and fished the gold chain out of the bilge. I saw Rigaberto's eyes widen when I brought it back. "He was crazy—but not too crazy to find this. He wanted me to keep it for him. He was going to pick it up when he got back to Key West."

"And you say he had found some coins too, huh?"

"Yeah. I found them at his camp the next day. They were hidden in some kind of pine tar or something. But I couldn't find Giff. If he got into trouble that same day, his tent and the coins still should be there on the beach."

Rigaberto made a final note and stood up. "We'll have the Coast Guard take a look." He and Norm shook hands, and he parted without trying to pry into what business a federal agent had with me. He was sharp enough not to ask.

"Seems like a good man," Norm said after Rigaberto had left.

"They don't come any better. And that was a good idea you had about offering him a job. From what I've seen and read, our dear government is having a hard time coming up with competent people."

"Now, Dusky, you aren't going to go into one of your tirades about the government, are you? I remember meeting you in the jungle for the first time, and for a week I thought you were strictly a 'yes sir, no sir' guy until that night when we were both off duty and I happened to mention the Republican party."

"And you didn't mention it kindly, as I remember."

"That's true! And, after that, I thought I had you figured out—until I mentioned the Democratic party. And then I realized you were just a goddam independent who doesn't like the idea of anybody controlling anybody else."

"You got it. Sure you don't want a beer, Norm?"

He thought for a moment. "No, let's wait until we've finished talking. And then I'll be off duty. Officially."

"So you are here on business?"

He glared at me. "You're one sly bastard, you know that? Trap an old friend like that."

"Take it easy, take it easy. So what's up?"

Norm paused for a moment, thinking. "Well, I'm not really sure, Dusky."

"It doesn't have anything to do with the old man who disappeared, does it? I noticed the way you suddenly started paying attention."

Norm motioned with his hand reflectively. "I don't think so. Probably just a coincidence. But we do need someone out in the Marquesas–Dry Tortugas area. Not much to it, really. You know that the shrimping industry is big business these days."

I nodded. It certainly was. After a minimum initial investment of $100,000 for boat, nets, supplies, and crew, a working man could go out and make a decent living—if he knew how to work the drags and where to work the drags, and if the weather didn't blow him into financial ruin. For the small businessman it had become a winner-take-all gamble. For the corporations that had plenty of capital for a slow-return investment, it was a surefire moneymaker. Big business all the way.

"What about it?" I said.

"Well, we're seeing more and more foreign vessels in our waters. That's not that unusual, really. Our shrimpers work around the Florida coast, up around Texas, and then down into Mexico and

South America. Their shrimpers do the same, and so do the Cubans. There have been some minor boundary squabbles—they arrest some of our people, and we arrest some of theirs—all depending on the political atmosphere at that particular time. But mostly, everyone just turns his head and ignores the minor infringements."

"That much I already know."

"Well, it's probably nothing at all, but lately there's been one particular Cuban shrimp boat hanging around on the Marquesas. They've been fishing, but they seem to keep working the same area over and over again."

"Maybe they're after the treasure Gifford Remus was after?"

"That would make things nice and neat—but it just doesn't figure. They've been working a couple of miles offshore where the water's too deep for a scuba diver—especially a fifty-some-odd-year-old scuba diver. Another thing is, salvaging Spanish treasure is a little too flashy and chancy for a communist-controlled government. When they make an investment, they want a profit in return, no ifs, ands, or buts about it. I'm not saying they wouldn't go after treasure if they thought it was a sure thing."

"This is no sure thing, Norm. People have been hunting the *Gaspar* for years. And even if they did find it, it would take them months, maybe a whole year, to do a proper salvage job."

"Right. And there's no way they could try it in our waters without us catching on."

"So what do you figure they're doing?"

He shifted in his booth seat. "We're not sure,

obviously. That's why I'm here talking to you. But
the only thing that makes sense to me is that they're
working some kind of drug scam. Maybe the
shrimp boat is home base for a big delivery and
exchange system. Believe me, the Cuban government would be interested in that. They export
home-grown grass or cocaine—maybe even
heroin—and rake in big American bucks through
a stateside connection."

"Why don't you just close in and search them?"

"We did. Once. Found nothing but crates of iced
shrimp. We could have made a federal case out
of it—Cuban shrimp boat in American waters. But
that would have just made it tough on our American shrimpers when they happened to get a little
too close to Castro's little island in the sun. So we
need someone with a cover to go out there and
keep an eye on them. Nothing obvious. Just watch
and let us know if you see anything unusual."

"For how long?"

"A week. Two weeks. Whatever it takes."

He sensed my disinterest. "Not exciting enough
for you?"

"I just got back from vacation, Norm. I don't
need another one. Why don't you just use high-
flying reconnaissance planes or something?"

"We have been. And we'll continue to do so
until they either leave or we find out just what in
the hell it is they're doing. But we want someone
out there, too. Look, Dusky, when you agreed to
work for us you had to know it wouldn't be all
excitement; just a handy little ploy to get your
revenge and keep your own ass out of jail. You
have to take the good with the bad. We need a

local man out there, and you happen to be the
only local man we have."

Some choice. "You're quite a salesman, Stormin'
Norman. So what's my cover? I rarely get two-
week charters."

He laughed good-naturedly. "I can't do all your
thinking for you, Captain. You decide."

So I decided. There was one cover I could use
that would allow me to keep an eye on the Cu-
banos and maybe find out a thing or two about
the disappearance of Gifford Remus, all at the
same time. I went to the beer locker and got a
cold one for me and another for my now off-duty
friend. And then I sat down and explained how I
was about to turn treasure hunter.

6

There was only one problem with my trying to pose as a treasure hunter: I don't know a damn thing about hunting treasure.

So what do you do when you don't know something? You go to the public library, pick up enough background information to ask sensible questions, and then you talk to the people who *do* know.

The public library in Key West is a stately building with an atmosphere of histrionic grace. In general, the librarians are in love with their jobs, in love with the island, and they are anxious to help anyone who shows the slightest interest in history or adventure—two subjects which seem to go hand in hand in Key West. My librarian was a blond woman in her fifties who smiled as if she knew some wonderful secret no one else could possibly know. Blue eyes, handsome aged face, and severe and maidenly clothing.

"You say you would like some information on

treasure hunting in Key West? Hmm. . . ." She smiled. This was, apparently, no unusual request.

"Treasure hunting in Florida, ma'am."

She shook her head. "No, no, you musn't call me 'ma'am.' Please. It sounds so . . . so *old*. And librarian-like. My name is Ann. Or Mrs. Tschillard."

"I think I'll choose 'Ann.' And I'm Dusky. I'll tell you exactly what I'm looking for, Ann. Technical data. How to hunt treasure; what equipment you'll need. Stuff like that."

She put a finger to pursed lips, thinking momentarily. "I really don't know of anything we have in one volume that could help you. But we do have files on treasure and treasure hunting— much of it cross-referenced to microfilm."

"That's fine."

She walked me back through the long stacks, sat me at a table, and put the promised files before me. "Happy treasure hunting, Dusky," she whispered.

"If I strike it rich, I'll give you ten percent."

She winked and went back about her duties. Must be a pleasant job for the intellectual types or the romantic types. The whole world is at your fingertips; all the adventure and intrigue, complete with statistics, catalogued in a fashion as orderly as Mr. Dewey's decimals will allow it.

So I went through the data, skimming for technical words; stuff I could use to convince the people with whom I might talk that I was indeed a serious treasure hunter. And there were plenty of data. I had no idea so much treasure had been found in Florida. There were, of course, the fa-

mous names: Kip Wagner and Mel Fisher. Together and separately they had found thousands
of pounds of lost Spanish gold and silver. They
had run amazingly large and complex treasure-
finding organizations on a shoestring, both of
them displaying remarkable ingenuity. Using
makeshift equipment at first, they invented or
jury-rigged the gear that wasn't available or that
they couldn't afford. There were plenty of ac-
counts of other treasure hunters, too—none of
them as successful as Wagner and Fisher, but all
as persistent. Through personal losses, deaths, and
other tragedies, they pushed on. Treasure was the
thing. And find it at any cost.

I spent the morning reading and taking notes.
Ann stopped back by to make sure I had everything I needed. She brought me coffee, began to
leave, and then hesitated.

"Dusky?"

"Yes, Ann."

"I hope you don't mind my prying, but I've
always wondered just what it is that makes people
so . . . so crazy about hunting treasure." It wasn't
a rebuke. She stood by my little table, eyes quizzical. It really was something she couldn't
understand.

And I couldn't understand it either. But in my
role as treasure hunter, I had to try.

"Money is one thing. There are millions of dollars out there, just waiting to be found."

She nodded. "Oh, yes, I know that—but there
seems to be something more to it. You have no
idea how many requests we get for the information you have there. Requests from all over the

nation. Ohio, Iowa, Indiana—people write or visit from all over, and they all want to hunt for treasure.''

''Well, just for the record, there really aren't that many who actually search—not seriously, anyway. According to what I've just read here, there are probably only forty or fifty active treasure hunters in Florida. Quite a few, I agree. But not that many when you consider the thousands who are interested. I guess for the ones who just read about it, treasure hunting offers some sort of vicarious adventure. You know, armchair thrill seekers. They'll write for information and plan their expeditions, but nothing will ever come of it—because they don't want anything to come of it. They probably wouldn't admit it to themselves, but I suspect they actually invent insoluble problems—financial or other—to keep them home.''

She nodded quickly. ''Oh, I know that. In fact— and it's terribly hard to admit it—I'm rather like that myself. But what about the other ones—the people like you? The men who actually go out and search for it?''

That was a hard one. I had never really met any of the big-time treasure hunters. But I knew plenty of the small-time operators. I tried to piece what I knew of them and what I had read together. ''You don't mind a little more armchair psychoanalysis?''

She smiled. ''Of course not.''

''Okay. First of all, treasure hunters—at least the ones I know—are not particularly pleasant people. They seem to be rather snobbish—no, I guess 'exclusive' is a better word—about what they do and what they know. Treasure hunting seems to make them feel rather intimate with history and boats and the sea; almost as if in finding treasure lost two or three hundred years ago, they can rightfully make claim to the sea itself. The hunt seems to provide them with a sense of exclusivity. But instead of making them very noble or romantic, it seems to make them very selfish instead. Does that make any sense?"

She thought for a moment. "Yes, it does—everything but hearing it from you. I'm afraid you don't seem either snobbish or selfish."

"Give me a chance to find something," I said. "I expect to become the biggest jerk around as soon as I find something."

And the nice librarian, Ann, went off chuckling after I had promised to ask for only her if I needed to do more research.

It was lunchtime in Key West. Store employees sat on street benches eating their sandwiches, and the druggies moved through the pale October sunlight in ragged pods, like leaves in slow-motion dust devils. The streets were slow and filled with light and life. Scenic Key West. Indian town, pirate town, fisherman's town, Navy town, and now tourist town. Sometimes I wonder why I stay.

I was hungry myself, so I stopped at my favorite restaurant—El Cacique—and found I didn't even have to order. I took my regular seat at the bar and drank the good Crystal beer, waiting for my fried snapper, black beans, and yellow rice to arrive. I saw Rigaberto Herrera sitting toward the rear of the crowded restaurant and caught his eye.

He waved for me to join him, so I picked up my beer and took a seat.

"I thought you were on a diet, Dusky."

"I am. But I just can't seem to keep away from this place."

Rigaberto had a little demitasse of espresso. He gulped half of it and went to work on his own lunch: some kind of pork cooked with onions and citrus, rice, tossed salad, and fried bananas.

He cut up his meat in neat bite-size pieces, one by one, before he started the entrée, and grabbed some more Cuban bread from the red plastic basket on the table. "Diets! How I hate diets, my friend. Luckily, I don't have to worry anymore. I've become a part of the latest national fad."

"Roller skating," I said incredulously.

He smirked. "No, you gringo fool. Jogging. I'm almost embarrassed to admit it, but it's true. My wife again. God, why did I have to marry a saint?"

He shoved huge forkfuls of food into his mouth dejectedly, his eyes a parody of resignation. "I just happened to mention to her that I wanted to get back in shape. In Cuba, *amigo,* I was in excellent condition—"

"Running from Castro's forces?"

"Hah! That's not even funny! No, I was in excellent shape because I played soccer. A fine sport—much tougher than our American football."

"I'd like to hear you discuss that with an NFL linebacker."

He ignored my prodding and went on. "So my wife, she says, 'I've been jogging a mile or two each night. Why don't you join me this evening?' "

"How long ago was that?"

"Three weeks ago! It's terrible. The faster I get, the faster she gets." Rigaberto banged his glass down on the restaurant table hard enough to draw the attention of nearby diners. "But I will not give up! It may take me a year, but her time will come! I will yet prove the superiority of the Cuban male. That I swear."

My friend ignored my laughter and returned his attention to his lunch. And when my food came, I too turned my full energy to the task at hand. I don't know how they do it, but the Cubans have a way of frying snapper that makes it a delight beyond description. And add to the snapper a helping of black beans and yellow rice, fresh Bermuda onion, and plenty of fresh lime, and you have a meal that is truly addictive. Rigaberto called for more espresso, then sat back and watched me finish my lunch.

"By the way, Dusky, I contacted the Coast Guard. I told them about Gifford Remus's camp."

I took a cold sip of the good Crystal beer. "Any word back?"

He shook his head. "I'll give you a call at the marina when I hear something. But to tell you the truth, I don't know if anyone is going to have much time to put into an investigation. It's sad to say, but one old man's disappearance from a small boat doesn't constitute a top-priority crime." He saw the look in my eye and added hastily, "Don't get mad at me, MacMorgan. I'm just telling you the truth. This damn island has gone crazy in the last few years. First the hippies came, and breaking-and-enterings suddenly tripled. And then drug-running became million-dollar business, and murders doubled. Now we have a massive number of homosexuals moving onto the island—they think it's a quaint place, I guess— and the local rednecks have all but declared war on them. Christ, this place is getting worse than New York City, and no small law-enforcement agency, no matter how good—and we are pretty good, I think—can take care of it all. I'm just saying that it would be a lot easier if Gifford Remus just happened to hit a coral head or something and drowned. Because I doubt if it's going to go any farther."

I was about to make some cutting reply when a commotion at the front part of the restaurant caught our attention. Funny how someone can raise a loud voice in laughter in a crowded bar or restaurant, and no one notices. But the softest exchange in anger silences everyone, and the emotion moves across the place in a wave. And that's what was happening now.

There was a table of them: five clean-cut sunburned but rugged-looking tourist types. Four of them looked to be in their early twenties. Blond hair, broad shoulders, all wearing gym shorts, Topsiders, and the kind of T-shirts they sell at the tourist traps. They looked like the backfield of some Midwestern high school football team that had come to Key West to celebrate graduation. The fifth man at the table was an older carbon copy of the others—but he had bright copper-colored hair and, with his red beard and film-perfect Nordic features, looked like a Viking. They all sat with their heads slightly bent, flushed and nervous, while a sixth man—a giant of a Creole-looking guy with greasy, shoulder-length black hair, pocked face, dirty khaki pants and a brutal-looking fillet knife strapped to his waist—berated them in a low voice of rage. In the sudden silence of the restaurant I could hear snatches of their bitter conversation.

"You screwed me, man. You ain't gonna get away with it. . . ."

"I'm sorry . . . I really am. I had no idea . . ." The man with the copper hair and red beard looked to be partly embarrassed and partly frightened by the encounter.

"Don't give me that innocent shit, man!" The black-haired giant edged closer, his hand on his knife. He spoke with some kind of strange accent—an accent I had never heard before.

"Look, I'll help you . . . I think we can reason this out like human beings. . . ."

The voice was still kept low, but it was harsher now. "Screw your reason. I no go to the law—this the kind of reason I'll give you. . . ."

Rigaberto and I were already moving from the table when the huge Creole reached for his knife, pulling it from its sheath in a wide sweeping arc that almost connected with the throat of the man with the red beard. It was in my mind that the knife thrust was not intended to kill—only to intimidate—but before I had time to get to the table and stop the black-haired aggressor, red beard was already out of his chair. He caught the

giant's arm as it finished its arc, chopped down
on the exposed elbow with the cutting edge of his
right hand. There was a loud *crack* like the sound
of a frozen tree limb snapping, and then red beard
jerked the giant around so they stood back to
back, and with one swift motion cradled the huge
man's head in a vise of forearm and bicep, twisting down and away. There was another loud *crack*:
this one moist, hollow-sounding, lethal.

"Hold it! Police!" It was Rigaberto. He held his
badge in one hand, his snub-nosed .38 in the
other. Diners in the restaurant were suddenly in
wild   disarray: women   screamed,   someone
dropped a tray of cups and saucers. The man with
the red beard looked stunned, then horrified.

"Oh my God," he said. "Oh my God . . ."

Strangely, the four young men, in apparent
shock, had not moved from the table. They looked
as if they still waited for their orders to come:
mild, expectant.

Rigaberto leaned over the fallen giant, checking
pulse and pupils. "Someone call an ambulance!"
he yelled.

The red-haired man took a step forward. Sitting
at the table, I had underestimated his own size.
He was rugged-looking, all right: massive shoulders, fists like hams, and a corded wrestler's neck.
The fallen Creole had, obviously, done some un-
derestimating of his own. "He's not . . . not dead,
is he?" The man truly looked upset, like a kid—
unfamiliar with his own strength—who has
crushed a baby rabbit.

"I think he's dead," said Rigaberto roughly,

"but I'm no doctor. Did somebody get hold of the emergency squad?"

People behind the counter scrambled. "There's one on its way now!"

Rigaberto closed the dead man's eyes with his fingertips and stood up, shaking his head. I mouthed the letters "CPR?" After all, it wouldn't hurt to try some first aid.

"Neck's broken," Rigaberto said softly. He turned to red beard, who still seemed horrified by what he had done. There are too many of them on the streets now, you know—the YMCA karate experts. They practice their deadly "hobby" once, twice, three times a week while old ladies in adjoining rooms knit or take disco lessons. They know lethal combat only as the fight scene in some old John Wayne movie. Well, red beard's lessons had suddenly paid off. He now stood as a perplexed victor over the corpse of an adversary.

"I . . . I can't believe it. I didn't want to *kill* him. . . ."

"What's your name?" Rigaberto asked him.

"Boone," the man said in a monotone, still looking at the body. The giant lay belly down, his head at a grotesque angle, almost facing the ceiling. "Jason Boone."

"And where are you from, Mr. Boone?"

"What? Oh . . . Davenport, Iowa. I'm the leader of an amateur underwater archaeology club. We've been down here for . . ." He turned to the four young men at the table. "About three weeks?" They all nodded. "Yes, three weeks."

Rigaberto sighed, covered his mouth, and repressed a belch. Poor cops. They can never get away from it. Bedtime, lunchtime, Christmas day, and the rest, they can never escape the wide swath of violence which moves through this nation daily. The cops are our protectors, our buffer zone from reality. And what do they get for it? Bad pay, bad hours and screams of "Brutality, brutality!" when they finally do snap under the pressure and make a mistake. "Mr. Boone, there's no doubt you were simply acting in self-defense, but I'm afraid you're going to have to go down to the office anyway. Just a formality. I'm going to stay here and finish up—get names of some witnesses, and so on—so perhaps Mr. MacMorgan here would walk you down to the Sheriff's Department?"

He raised an eyebrow at me. I nodded.

"Your four friends here can go back to your motel or your boat—wherever it is you're staying. You won't be long."

Jason Boone bent over the table. Their lunches were still there, half-eaten. "If my wife happens to call from Davenport," he said, "please don't say anything about this. All right? I want to tell her in my own way."

We walked out onto the warm October streets of Key West. The tourists, what there were of them, moved by us in a happy flow. Outside Sloppy Joe's, a dirty young man of about twenty holding an equally dirty infant in his arms asked us for enough money to buy some Pampers for his daughter. The new breed of street merchants—they use brand names to give their line authenticity. Still in a daze, Boone reached into his pocket and handed the kid some change, then reached back in and handed him a twenty-dollar bill.

"Hey—thanks, man. Really. I . . . I mean, the kid is really going to be able to use this."

"You know that the last thing that money is going to go toward is a box of diapers, don't you?" I said as we walked on down Duval Street toward the Sheriff's Department.

"What?" Boone looked at me briefly, seeming to notice for the first time that I was there. "Oh, I didn't know . . . I . . ."

"It's one of the more common scams of the drug-culture kids here. Eight or ten of them will go in together and lease an old house. They all live there, sharing their food, their drugs, their women—everything. The young mothers more or less loan their children out to the guys so they can work the streets. Or, for effect, the mothers might come along. The lines vary: the child's sick and needs a doctor, or they need money to buy milk—or diapers. The woman and the guy split the take. It keeps the household in drugs."

Boone turned a hard eye at me. "You seem to be a very cynical man, Mr. . . . ?"

"MacMorgan. Dusky MacMorgan." I took his outstretched hand. He smiled a little sadly.

"After what happened back there, I suddenly feel cynicism to be an indulgence. A very costly indulgence. The cost is something quite precious—time. The man I . . . killed back there. Abbey . . ."

"Abbey?"

"Well, it was a nickname, I guess. His real name

was . . . well, some kind of Islamic name or something. I never really knew it. Anyway, his time was so short. It seems that for the first time in my life I really, truly know that." He shoved his hands in the pockets of his khaki fishing shorts. His head was bowed. I knew the sadness—that great, great weight of guilt and realization that settles upon you when you have stolen the life away from another human being. "And it was such a silly thing!" Boone continued. "Such a silly argument! God help me. . . ."

"Why was he mad at you?"

"What? Oh. I don't blame him, really—but we meant no harm. Our group—our amateur underwater archaeology club—worked for three long years to raise enough money to come down here and do some serious work. There are eighteen of us in all—many like those four young men back at the restaurant who had started with the club back when they were still in high school. We worked hard to get here, Dusky. Damned hard. I read everything I could about seventeenth- and eighteenth-century shipwrecks. I did my master's thesis on it at Iowa City. And the kids studied hard, too. Very dedicated—they're like young soldiers, the way they work and take orders. Such fine, serious kids. . . ."

"But what about the guy back at El Cacique? Abbey?"

Boone brushed his copper crew-cut with his right hand, thinking. "Abbey was a treasure hunter. We needed someone like Abbey—he had a boat, and a good working knowledge of the waters. And, frankly, he needed us. We would provide free manpower, the research, and some of the equipment. Legally, it was pretty complicated. But basically our deal was this: we would help him salvage any treasure we happened to find, and he would retain seventy-five percent of it—but we would do no salvaging until we had plotted the wreck and finished the archaeological work, which is really the only reason we're here. We aren't interested in treasure—it's knowledge we're after."

"That sounds like more than a fair deal to me—if anything, your people were being shorted."

"And we didn't mind, as long as he put us on some wreck sites. But as I said, it was rather complicated legally. To make sure Abbey held up his end of the bargain, I had a lawyer friend of mine draw up a contract. This was two months ago. I asked my friend only to make sure that, legally, Abbey couldn't take advantage of us. Some of these treasure hunters, you know, are something less than scrupulous. Well, my lawyer friend did a good job—too good a job. I mailed the contract off to Abbey. I assumed he had a lawyer read it over. He didn't. It turns out that the state permits for the various sites we were to work would be held only in the name of our club. Abbey would receive seventy-five percent of the treasure—but only that treasure which we deemed to be of no historical value. Obviously, my lawyer friend had put us in complete legal control. As I said, I don't blame him for being mad. Abbey was a very emotional man—the slave of his whims. Not an easy man to get along with. In shifts of six at a time, our whole group spent some very trying days

with him on that boat. God forgive me, I can't lie
and say that I liked the man. I didn't. But my
religion—everything I feel and believe in—forbids
me from hating any living thing. I didn't hate the
man, Dusky. But when he came at me with that
knife something deep within me snapped."

I put my hand on his shoulder. The poor bastard. He had never met the Creature before. The
Creature that rests dormant within the brains of
us all; the Creature that waits for the unsuspecting
moment to rush blood-ready to the surface and
prove that, even in the most intimate circumstances, we are all strangers, aliens even to ourselves. To take his mind off what had happened,
I asked him about his work. No, I'm lying. I didn't
ask just to relieve him of the burden of emotion.
The Creature within me demands an attempt, at
least, at honesty. He had information about
seventeenth- and eighteenth-century wrecks and
wreck sites, and I needed information. Some guy,
Dusky MacMorgan. Bleed the ailing; leech what
you need from the unsuspecting. I felt a thread of
guilt move through me even as I asked.

"What areas were you and your people
searching?"

He rubbed his forehead with a shaky hand.
"Hmm? Oh—the Boca Grande and Cosgrove
Shoal area, but I really can't . . ."

"Off the Marquesas?"

"Yes."

"Jason, I hope you take this in the way it's
meant. I'm interested in archaeology—I always
have been. Perhaps we could sit down over a beer
and you could give me the benefit—"

"Of course, of course, but please not now. My mind . . . I can't even think."

We were almost at the Sheriff's Department. I said nothing more. He was crying. . . .

7

As much as I liked the Hervey Yarbrough family, and as much as they had helped me in the past, I wasn't looking forward to eating dinner with them. The Yarbroughs are rarities in Key West—they are original Conchs. Natives. And they are proud of it. Hervey came from sailing captain stock; his forefather was the master of the old wrecking schooner *Orion*. His wife is a slightly pudgy woman who is always bustling around the house, always smiling wryly as if she understands some universal secret that no one but a mother and a wife could know. Both are good solid people; people with love and a sense of humor—people I would, and have, trusted with my life. But, frankly, Hervey's daughter, April, scares me just a little bit. No, not a little bit—a lot. April is an eighteen-year-old firebrand beauty with hip-length raven hair, and eyes that are puppy-sized, more golden than amber. I had known her since she was a barefooted kid playing in the dirt. And I had watched her grow up, smart and strong and independent as hell. She has a first-class mind, and a body that looks as if it was made for those ripe bikinis you see in magazines. And for some reason—sympathy after my wife was murdered, I guess—April got it into her head that I was the man destined for her. There is no coyness about the sure ones, the independent ones. She had come to my bed one night and made her intentions known so sincerely, so lovingly, that I had almost succumbed. But that's not why I am a little frightened of her. Aside from the more than fifteen-year age difference, she scares me because I know that, already a little in love with her, I could become so deeply and totally committed that it would ruin the life I know that awaits me. You cannot kill coldly, professionally, when you have something to live for. Loving me would only be her ruin.

Lights were on in the little clapboard tin-roofed house when I walked down the shell driveway. It was just after dusk, that soft time between night and day when the afterglow of sun is a burnished blue in the west, and the frail new moon is up in the east, putting the whole earth and its inhabitants in gentle balance. I could hear the cluck-a-cluck of roosting chickens in the long shed down by the docks. Boats groaned softly, shifting on their lines in the warm seawind. It was my favorite time of day. And for my best friend, Billy Mack, it had been a favorite time of day, too. After a hard charter, fishing for the big ones in the black-blue shimmer of the Gulf Stream, it was our practice to sit on the docks with a cold beer, waiting for this soft time in which to walk the streets

of Key West, home. Dusk. Billy Mack and I loved
the dusk. We had known it together in our Navy
SEAL training out in Coronado, California, and
we had known the dusk together in the jungled
hush of Vietnam and Cambodia, and we had
known it here in the Florida Keys. Together. Always together. An orphan, I think Billy was the
brother I never had. But no more. No more beer
after charters, and no more enjoying the dusk. My
wife, my best friend, my two fine, fine sons. Dead.
All dead. It's strange how a quality of light, the
sound of a distant voice, a half-imagined odor will
bring back so much; transport you from the present to a well-loved memory. Strange how your life
collapses, adjusts to change, and then clatters on;
clatters on like old photographs rattling in some
forgotten box, or like a mobile skeleton, driven
but empty. So in that nice time of day, I clattered
on up the drive toward the little house. I could
smell meat frying, and the acid hint of collard
greens. I started to whistle—probably a mistake.
The Yarbroughs are under the guardianship of a
big, yellow-eyed Chesapeake Bay retriever they
called Gator. Hervey likes to tell the story. He had
been bass fishing up on Lake Trafford in the
south-central part of Florida. He was wading the
banks, plug casting. It was misty, just after sunrise, and he noticed something swimming at him
through the arrow plants.

"Thought it was a big ol' bull gator. But it
weren't. Was this anvil-headed dog here—and he
was *carryin'* a four-foot gator in his mouth. Thing was
still squirmin'. Dog was lost, near starved, with no
collar or nothin'—he'd taken to eatin' gators for a

livin'. They'd swim up thinkin' to eat him, an' he'd jes' swim out an' turn the tables. Never seen no dog swim better—atop the water, ten feet under the water. Didn't matter to him. Well sir, he finished part o' that gator's tail, picked up the rest, and jumped in my truck. I had no say in matters. He's owned us ever since."

That Chesapeake acted as if he owned the Yarbroughs, all right. When I started to whistle, he came roaring out of the new darkness; ninety pounds of head, yellow eyes, and muscle.

"*Gator!* Gator, dammit—it's a friend!"

When he started to slow down, I knew I was okay. If he hadn't recognized me, he would have speeded up. A porch light blinked on.

"Dusky? Hey, that you out there?" The bulky figure of Hervey squinted out from the doorway. "That dog knows you; come on up."

Inside, Hervey's wife, Flora, leaned over the stove, hands moving every direction at once.

"Food'll be ready in a short," she yelled happily. "Hope you like pork chops and greens, Dusky. Jus' threw it together, an' Lord knows if it'll be any good."

Hervey and I took seats in the living room, with glasses of iced tea. The chairs were threadbare but comfortable. The floor was covered with a throw rug.

"Chew?" Hervey had his ever-present foil packet of Red Man, and a brass spittoon sat squatly beside his easy chair. "Nothing like a chew with a glass o' tea before dinner."

So we made small talk, taking turns at the brass cuspidor. Yes, I had fixed the bow rail on my

Sniper. Screws worked fine. Yes, the fishing was getting worse every year, and the canal and condominium barons had screwed up the drainage system of that great sweeping river of grass called the Everglades. Too much fresh water in Florida Bay now. Salinity was off, and the fish were disappearing: the effect felt clear down in Key West. Yes, federal officials, working in cahoots with their lamebrain advisers, had tried to correct the problem back-asswards. Instead of making the developer big-money boys correct the problem for which they were responsible, they outlawed commercial fishing in national park coastal areas—putting many of the small-time net fishermen out of business. Money shouts, politicians tremble, and we suffer. When the time was right, I asked Hervey if he knew anything about a treasure hunter named Abbey.

He tugged at his bushy black beard. "Hmm . . . What's his last name?"

"I don't know yet. It's supposed to be Islamic."

Hervey spit. "Hard to keep up on all the foreigners coming into the island. Naw, ain't heard of him. Most them other treasure hunters I do know about, though. Tough bunch. Always runnin' around like they was carryin' secrets. Like them gold prospectors you see in them western movies. Someone gets too close to their claim, a boat gets blown up mysteriously. One o' their men gets drunk an' does a bit too much talkin', next thing he knows he's on a plane bound for Dubuque. That question got anything to do with ol' Gifford Remus?"

"I don't think so. I'm going to level with you, Hervey. I talked to a friend of mine at the Sheriff's Department just before I came. I'd told him about seeing Gifford when I was off the Marquesas, and I told him where the Coast Guard could find Gifford's camp. But when the Coast Guard checked into it, everything was gone. No tent, no pottery, no Spanish coins."

"You think it's murder, then?"

I thought for a moment. "Could be. Anyway, I'm going to run my boat out there and have a look. Too much other stuff going on for the regular law-enforcement people to give it much time, so—"

I was interrupted by the screen door swinging shut. It was April, as striking as ever, even in the white waitress uniform she wore. "Well, well, well," she said, hands on her hips, "look who's back from vacation!" Ludicrously, I found myself standing at her entrance, gentleman-like. Hervey, the bastard, just sat and smirked.

"You recognize this big mean-lookin' character?" Hervey said, playing devil's advocate.

"Why yes, Papa, I believe I do." She smiled what seemed to be a soft, honest smile, came up to me and gave me a sisterly hug. "You don't come round nearly as often as you should, Dusky—you know how much Mama and ol' Papa here enjoy seein' you." She smiled sweetly again and headed for her room, calling over her shoulder, "I'll be back after I clean up to help, Mama!"

I sat back down. Hervey wagged his eyebrows. "Seems jes' gentle as a lamb, don't she? Well, you just wait, mister man. She ain't gonna let you off *that* easy. Believe me, I know that girl." He leaned back in his chair, laughing. "Yes sirree!"

"For God's sake, Hervey, why don't you try to talk some sense into your daughter's head? I'm almost twenty years older than her—dammit, I'm old enough to be her father."

"Wait a minute there now, Dusky." Hervey waved toward the kitchen. "That ain't what you'd call a good excuse around this house. I'm near fifteen year older than my old woman out there— never bothered us. Had an uncle once who married a girl from Immokalee who weren't but fifteen—an' he was forty-six."

April came out of her room. She looked at us wryly and gave her hip-length raven hair a toss. "My, my, my," she said. "How you men folk do gossip!"

The dinner was Southern cooking at its best, complete with hot corn bread and butter. But I forced myself to eat sparingly—not because the food wasn't good, but because, for me, it was discipline time. Stormin' Norman Fizer hadn't given me much of a mission, but it was still a mission, and for me, getting back in shape after a few weeks of drinking beer and lounging around the boat is a tedious process. It means easy on the alcohol and starches. And heavy on the running, swimming, and pull-ups. At six-two, 215, a six-minute mile is about the best I can do—six and a half minutes is acceptable. In the best of shape, I can do thirty-six backhanded pull-ups, and this morning I could only do twenty-four. So it was discipline time. I needed work, because you never, never know. . . .

April was waiting outside after I had thanked Flora Yarbrough for the dinner and made my excuses for an early exit. I knew she would be there. She stood in the shadows of a massive banyan tree that scattered its air roots across the dirt lawn. She held something in her hand, and when I got closer I could see that it was a stalk of jasmine, the flowers white in the shadows of her hands.

"Good supper, huh, April?"

She pulled at the petals of the flowers, dropping them by her bare feet. "Couldn't tell by the way you ate—hardly enough for a bird, if you ask me."

I put my hands on her shoulders and felt her sag slightly at my touch. "April, I'm sorry you're mad at me."

"Who says I'm mad?" She pulled away, turning her back. In the pale moonlight, her long hair looked blue-black, the color of the Gulf Stream at dusk. There was a long silence. And then:

"Was your blond New York woman prettier than me, Dusky?"

"No, April. It wasn't that."

"Dusky, you tol' me once—after your wife died—that if there was ever another woman it was to be me. . . ."

"And I also told you that you're far too young, April."

"Do you love her, Dusky? That other woman?" She stood facing me, looking up into my face with her golden eyes.

"In a way, yes. I did, but I never told her. . . ."

She trembled, struggling, then dropped the jasmine and fell into my arms, crying. "I'm so worried about you, Dusky. You've made up your mind 'bout something and it ain't good. You got to quit punishin' yourself; you gettin' killed ain't gonna bring your family back. . . ."

I held her away from me and tried to smile. "Whoa . . . wait a minute, girl. Just what is it you're talking about?"

She wiped her eyes angrily and sniffed. "Don't lie to me, you big ape! I heard you tellin' Papa that you're leavin' in your boat to look for some murderer or somethin'."

"Eavesdropping, huh?"

"Yes!"

"And you don't want me to go?"

She flipped her hair at me and started walking down toward the dock. The big Chesapeake came up beside her, and she scratched his head while he sighed heavily, content. I followed along behind. "Dusky," she said, "I want you to do anything you want to do. I ain't one to whine an' complain like some women. I just worry about you, that's all." She stopped by the water and turned to look at me again. "Dusky, I'm just afraid that if you leave on that boat, I ain't never gonna see you again."

"April . . ."

"No, I mean it, Dusky. I had this dream—three times I had it. I was in a hospital, and you was hurt; hurt real bad." She lifted her hand and touched my face, and I could smell the jasmine she had held. "You had a bandage wrapped around your head—right here. And I was cryin' 'cause I knew I was never going to have you . . . never, ever. . . ."

I took her in my arms, holding the soft warmth of her as she cried. The poor, poor sweet girl. But maybe she was right. I thought about it, standing in the darkness by the water. Maybe it was a little silly to give up all desire for a rational life. And if I ever was to join in marriage with another woman, how could I do any better than April? Lee Johnson? Lee was a good woman, a strong yet tender person, but we came from different worlds. And there was her husband. . . . I turned back to April and for a moment—one long, compelling moment—I considered it. April, a young new wife, a new home and babies again—maybe two more sons. Forget the past and start over. But then I felt the hatred in my brain move from the depths like a slashing pain. And I knew it was futile. I had a new master now. Revenge.

"April," I said, "listen to me. Everyone has dreams. Good dreams, bad dreams—but those dreams don't necessarily forecast what is to be. I'm just going out to the Marquesas for a week— two weeks at the most. For a friend. And if there is to be any rough stuff—which there won't be— I'm going to go for help so fast it would surprise even you."

It was supposed to be funny. It was supposed to put her at ease and make her smile. But it didn't. She backed away from me and said with great seriousness, "Dusky, please . . . please don't ever lie like that to me again." She put her finger to my lips when I started to speak. "I know you're doing it as a kindness. But if I can't be your wife, or . . . or your lover, I want to be your friend. You weren't built for tellin' lies, an' I wasn't built to listen to them."

I lifted her face gently and kissed her softly on her full lips. "You're some woman, April Yarbrough."

She smiled for the first time. "I've been tryin' to tell you that, Mr. Dusky MacMorgan. Now this time, before you leave, kiss me just once like you really, truly mean it. And promise me you'll come back. . . ."

8

If you want to meet with D. Harold Westervelt, you have to pick your time—and make sure your time coincides with a break in his stern order of habit and discipline. D. Harold Westervelt. *Colonel* D. Harold Westervelt. He is one of my more unusual friends. We had both survived military life and war, commando raids and espionage missions, but where I had married and found a new life as a fishing guide, Colonel Westervelt could never leave it behind. He loved it all too well. He lives in an ironically peaceful setting: a stucco suburban house near the naval airbase on Boca Chica Key. When he got too old for predawn assaults, the War Department kept him on the Army payroll as a sort of freelance inventor and adviser. They financed his sometimes strange notions and, in return, he produced for them highly sophisticated—although sometimes unusual—weaponry. And when Norm Fizer's federal agency retained me for an entirely different type of freelance work, Colonel Westervelt had doubled as my friend and armorer. On my first mission, if it hadn't been for his advice and his weapons . . . well, let's just say that after one world war, one police action, and then Vietnam, D. Harold Westervelt knows what he is talking about.

The morning after my dinner with the Yarbroughs I awoke, as always, at first light. Since the death of my family I had abandoned our little house on Elizabeth Street and set up household in my sportfisherman, *Sniper*. It is a perfect big-game boat: thirty-four-feet of custom-built, long-range, oceangoing craftsmanship. And equipped just the way I wanted it. There's the Si-Tex/Koden 707 digital readout Loran C, the Furuno FE-502 whiteline commercial fish finder, a Konel VHF marine radio, the Si-Tex radar system, and an enormous fuel capacity for a range of over four hundred miles plus safety factor. But as I konked my knee stepping into the head for my morning duties, I realized for the umpteenth time that, as much as I loved my boat, it might not be the ideal home for a guy my size. It was built as a fishing machine, not as an apartment.

What then? Buy another house? No, never again . . .

I considered the options as I slipped into soft gym trunks and, with my shaving kit, headed barefooted along the cement dock toward the marina to shower and try to call D. Harold. In the trash cans along the dock, there were carcasses of filleted dolphin and wahoo, green flies already busy around them. As I passed his rickety beige houseboat, *Fred Astaire*, Stevie Wise hailed me from the forward deck.

"Hey! Hey, Dusky—you coming to my party tonight?" He wore nothing but white BVD's, and he already had a mug of beer in his hand. Behind him in a big red garbage bucket was a keg of beer. He lifted his glass to me. "Plenty more where this came from. Stop by if you get a chance." As he spoke, a sleepy-eyed dishwater blond with nothing but a towel around her poked her head out the door. "Stevie? Where did you say the shower was?"

Stevie smiled at me and winked. He was happy again.

After shaving and brushing my teeth, I made my phone call. It's twenty-five cents in Key West now. When I'm grumpy I blame it on the Arabs. Fifteen rings and no answer. The Bell bandit gave me my quarter back when I hung up. He was working. D. Harold Westervelt always switched his phone off when he was in his lab. I checked my Rolex: not quite seven A.M. and he was already hard at it. People like D. Harold always make me feel even lazier than I am.

Workout time. I went back to my boat and pulled on my running shoes—the new kind with the yellow blaze stripe and the special foam rubber soles guaranteed to keep your legs from aching. Only my legs always ache when I run—the Japanese manufacturers failed to consider, obviously, the possibility of shrapnel wounds. Down busy Roosevelt Boulevard past the Kangaroo's Pouch, the floating restaurant where boat people were already filing in for breakfast, turn right on Palm Avenue, across the little causeway. Wave at an old friend at Steadman's Boat Yard, smile through the sweat and the ache at the early-morning children.

Look, Mommy! Did you see that funny man wink at me?

Curve left at Eaton past the old shipbuilders' houses, then down into the heart of Old Town. Old Town has a case of the quaints these days. Shop owners, in a desperate attempt to please the tourists, are trying to make Key West look like New Orleans—and failing. Too much ornamentation, too many cutesy signs. Avoid Elizabeth Street, avoid El Cacique with its tempting morning odor of espresso, push on, push on, don't even stop to comfort and scratch the ears of the poor stray dogs. The sun felt good on my shoulders, sweat dripping down into my eyes, and when Roosevelt Boulevard came into view again, I kicked it into high gear, checking my watch before I hit the last mile. Huffing and puffing like an overweight ex-jock at one of those Sunday softball games, I pulled up at the marina. Three seven-and-a-half minute miles and a final seven-minute mile. I punished myself with grim accusations: *too fat, too old, too slow, slow, slow. . . .* I got a towel from the port locker, got a drink of cold water from the little refrigerator, then punished myself some more with a hundred slow pull-ups, sets of fifteen. The average human spends adolescence getting to know his or her body, the next ten years primping and grooming it, and the final unknown decades alternately abusing it and castigating it. (*Just one more whiskey before I go to the hospital to check on this damn liver problem I got. . . .*) I smiled at the silliness of us all.

After showering, I tried D. Harold once more and got my quarter back. I checked my watch. He'd be breaking for lunch in about two hours. So I ambled back to my boat, got an icy beer from the fridge, and sat in a salon chair doing some mental exercise. Fact: one Gifford Remus, after making what was an apparently significant treasure discovery, had disappeared. Question: Did he die accidentally, was he murdered, or was he being held by someone? Fact: A Cuban shrimp boat was in that same area under suspicious circumstances. Question: Was it the staging site for some communist drug-smuggling operation? Was it on some sort of spy mission? Was the disappearance of Remus in any way related to its presence? Or perhaps it *was* just a shrimp boat honestly, if not innocently, engaged in the common business of fishing outside its own waters.

Fact . . . question . . . fact . . . I sat drinking my beer in the fresh morning heat building plausible and complex schemes which would explain it all. But as Watson's detective once said, it is a capital mistake to hypothesize before all the data are available. So I let it rest. At lunchtime I would go to see my friend the colonel, announced or unannounced. He would have more information. And it was too important to wait.

Just as I was locking up the *Sniper*, ready to head off toward Colonel Westervelt's home, I had a visitor. A stock blond young man, about twenty, dressed in khaki shorts and T-shirt, came up and knocked on the piling at the stern.

"Mr. MacMorgan?"

"Dusky MacMorgan. That's right."

He was a nice-looking kid—the kind you see on the cover of *Boys' Life*. And polite, too. You don't see many polite ones anymore. I think they went out with radio theater. "Permission to come aboard, sir?"

"Sure. Absolutely." I checked my watch. "But I'm afraid I can't give you much time."

"It won't take long, sir." He stepped down onto the deck nimbly and offered me his hand. Firm grip but not overbearing. Dry palm. I had seen him someplace before, and it took me a moment to place him. El Cacique. He had been with Jason Boone, the amateur underwater archaeologist, when the lethal fight had broken out.

"How's your friend Jason doing, ah . . ."

"Wayne, sir. My name's Wayne Peters."

"And my name's Dusky, not 'sir.' So how's your friend doing, Wayne?"

He cleared his throat a little uncomfortably. "It was awful, what happened, sir . . . I mean, Dusky. Jason's not a violent man; not since he accepted Christ as his savior, anyway. He's real religious, you see. In fact, God is the only thing that he takes more seriously than his work. So you can imagine what a blow it was to him."

"He seemed pretty upset."

"Well, he's a little better now. For a while there, he was talking about calling off the whole field trip and heading back to Iowa. Boy, I'd have hated that. I'm new to the group and all, and this is my first trip to the Keys, but I love it here. And between you and me, that Abbey character was one mean human being. If anybody deserved killing, he did."

"I take it you're not the devoted Christian that Jason is?"

He smiled the way old friends smile when they are conspiring. He had bright blue eyes and a fine, angular, Nordic face. "Well, I'm not as serious about it as some of the others. Besides, the Bible says, 'an eye for an eye, and a tooth for a tooth.' One evening on the boat, just off the Marquesas, I heard someone shouting up on the deck. I ran up and there was Abbey with one of those old Winchester .30-'06's—I recognized it because I used to use a rifle like it for deer hunting. Well, you know how porpoises will come and play around your boat when you're anchored? There were porpoises around our boat that night, and Abbey was shooting them just for sport. It made me sick."

The thought of it made me sick, too. I said, "I think I would have been tempted to stick that rifle up Mr. Abbey's ass."

Wayne smiled. "That's exactly what I told him I would do if he didn't stop."

"And?"

He lowered his eyes, suddenly embarrassed. "Wrestling's the state sport in Iowa, Dusky. By the time I was seventeen, I was an All-American at a hundred and sixty-five pounds. Abbey thought he could bully Jason because he's so religious, but he knew better than to mess with me. He stopped."

I listened to this kid and knew I liked him, but I was in a hurry. I checked my watch again.

"Look, I don't want to hold you up," he said hastily. "The reason I'm here is, Jason sent me. He wanted me to thank you for being so kind to him after the fight, and he wanted to invite you out to our motel. He said you were interested in underwater archaeology. We're staying at the Key Wester Inn. You know where it is?"

I nodded. "I'll probably be out in the morning. Okay?"

"Sure. We're headin' back out to sea in the afternoon, but the morning will be fine."

We shook hands again, and Wayne took his leave: broad-shouldered farm kid looking strangely out of place on this, the island of pirates. Before he got into his rental car, he called back over his shoulder, "I look forward to talking to you again sometime, Captain MacMorgan. I've heard a lot about you in the last couple of days."

Before I could ask him where he had heard about me and what, he was in the car, headed out of the marina parking lot, down Roosevelt.

D. Harold Westervelt was eating his spartan lunch of salad and unsweetened iced tea when I arrived. He was wearing swim trunks, and there was a towel around his neck. Every day, twice a day, he swims a strong half mile in the narrow, twenty-five-yard business-only pool beneath the bug screen on his patio. The blue water was still roiled as I took a seat across the table from him.

"So! You have another mission. I envy you." He made a sweeping motion with his right hand. "I've become a hermit here. When I was younger,

I never took the time to think how boring it must be to be an old soldier."

Colonel Westervelt looked like anything but an old soldier. He has icy blue eyes, the body of an Olympic-class gymnast, and a shaved head which makes his cranium seem disproportionately large—the general impression being that his brain is of the same quality as his body. An accurate impression, too. At some fifty-odd years of age, he is an impressive specimen.

I said, "I've always thought you were too busy to be bored, Colonel."

He gestured with his shoulders. "True, true. Yes, I have my laboratory and my work. But we are similar end products from different generations, Captain. There are a few of us left, but not many. You must understand how it is. Once you have had a mission, once you have seen combat with men under your command, everything else, in comparison, seems rather . . . bland."

I understood. All too well. And I wondered what I would be like if I lived to be D. Harold's age. Restless, lonely, and bored, bored, bored.

"Captain Fizer said you would have more information for me about our project."

"Of course." He finished his tea in a gulp, and I followed him down the hallway to the steel firedoor and his lab. He bolted the door behind us. Except for one wall lined with a marble workbench, there were chemicals, strange chunks of wood and plastic, and locked gun cabinets and relics from the Second World War everywhere. In the far corner, in an oblong glassed frame, his many decorations were pinned on blue velvet. The past and present of the consummate warrior all in one small room. As I looked about, D. Harold walked to the wall and pushed an unseen button. A small patch of workshop floor slid away with a cool hydraulic hiss, revealing a large gunmetal-colored floor safe. He twisted the dial, pulled the door open, and retrieved a brown folder marked "Top Secret" in bold type.

"Have you recovered from your last mission?" he asked as he leafed through the folder.

"Yes," I said. "Completely."

"That was a rather nasty head wound you had."

It was nasty all right. The spot was still tender, but the dizzy spells were less frequent now. "It's fine, sir," I said.

He pulled a workbench stool up and motioned for me to sit. "You know, after your assault on Cuda Key, there were people in high places who wanted to see you tried for mass murder." He smiled coldly. "But there were others who thought you ought to be decorated. I am continually amazed by the fools our voters put into office. The politicians don't realize that times of peace require the most relentless warfare of all. If you don't fight continually to preserve freedom, it slips away from you a grain at a time, leaving, in the end, a nation utterly drained and helpless."

"Have you—our people, I mean—heard anything more about the men who got away from Cuda Key?"

"That northern Senator, you mean."

Yes, I meant the Senator. He was the one who had masterminded the whole complex drug army

I had helped destroy. It was he who was responsible, directly or indirectly, for the deaths of my friend, my wife, and my sons. And I would hunt him until the day I died.

"The Senator has escaped to Argentina, I'm afraid. Strange country, Argentina. They have Nazis there, escaped dictators, revolutionary socialists in hiding, all living, apparently, healthy, wealthy, and wise. Strange bedfellows, most certainly."

I felt my knuckles whiten as I gripped my chair. I tried to make my voice flat, businesslike. "So there's no chance of extraditing him?"

"Oh, they're working on it through diplomatic channels, but I wouldn't put much faith in that. Frankly, there was some talk of sending one of our people over there to, ah . . . loosen things up."

"If you're looking for volunteers, I'd be happy—"

"All in good time, Captain. One mission at a time."

"But doesn't it seem a little silly for them to send me out to observe the habits of just one Cuban shrimp boat when I could be working on something really important like this—"

He held up his hand, shushing me. "When I was a young lieutenant, I was sent to a desolate sweep of beach with a handful of men on what seemed to be one more 'silly' recon mission. The name of that beach was Normandy, Captain. You never know. And you have your orders. Let's say nothing more about it."

Everything was in the file. High-altitude photos, the report made on the one search of the vessel.

The Cuban boat had obviously done some shrimping, slipping off the Tortugas to drag, but always returning to an area off the Marquesas to anchor.

"There's pathetically little to go on," said D. Harold after I had skimmed through the file. "For one thing, it might be completely innocent. For another thing—and I hate to say this—our intelligence people aren't as good as they once were. The information they give you is not always complete . . . or accurate. Some of them would be better off working for newspapers."

"The data was fed through the computers, I assume."

"Yes."

"Did it kick out any possible motive for the Cubans to place a vessel in our waters?"

"Several. It might be espionage. Their deep divers might be placing submarine radar-tracking devices on the bottom, camouflaging them as coralheads. Or nuclear explosives. Also, a very lethal grade of PCP—the kids call it angel dust, I believe—has been filtering into the national drug market through the Florida Keys. Perhaps they have something to do with that. Or they might be somehow smuggling cocaine or even heroin into the country, using the shrimp boat as the distribution center. The possibilities are nearly endless."

"Then why don't we just send out a squad of Marines and run them back to their own country."

"Oh, we plan to. But first we want to find out what they're up to."

D. Harold Westervelt went back to the floor safe and fished out another file. He handed me a paper. "For your cover as a treasure hunter, you will need this. It's a state permit to search a specific area of water immediately off the Marquesas Keys. You may leave that area, of course, but it would be best for appearance's sake if you spent most of your daylight hours there." He handed me another paper. "This is a list of the equipment I have requisitioned for you. The magnetometer is not of the kind normally used by treasure hunters. Rather than reacting to gold and silver and other metals, the one you will have is extremely sensitive to underwater electronic devices. The reason is obvious. For weaponry, I don't think you'll see anything on the list with which you are not familiar."

"Weapons?"

Colonel Westervelt smiled. "As I said, Captain— you never know." He handed me a thin folder. "You should also go over this before you leave. Any operation they might be carrying out short of espionage and honest fishing would require American connections. And the most likely suspects would be the people who frequent the Marquesas area. There's a list in there of people—treasure hunters, mostly—with a personal history when available. The boat I would watch most closely is the *Libertad*, a barge that has been converted into a treasure-salvage vessel by a group of Cuban-Americans."

I skimmed the list briefly, planning to go over it carefully later. But something under the name of Jason Boone caught my eye:

Capt. Green Berets, resigned commission Aug. '70;

Purple Heart (3), Silver Star, Bronze Star (2), Presidential citation for bravery in action Vietnam, April '69. . . .

Colonel Westervelt raised his eyebrows. "You've noticed something?"

"This fellow Jason Boone. I met him a few days ago."

"Yes, I heard something about that. Well, according to intelligence, the resignation of Captain Boone was a great loss to the American Army. They had big things planned for him. But he had some sort of a religious conversion or something and threw it all over for study."

"Odd," I said. "He seemed quite upset about killing a man who pulled a knife on him. I felt for sure that it must have been his first time."

"God does odd things to people, Captain. But if something happens out off the Marquesas, and you do get into a situation where you need help quick, intelligence has cleared Jason Boone for a partial briefing. Reborn Christian or not, he's a soldier. And if you need it, he'll help you."

"I doubt if I'll need it, but I'll keep him in mind."

D. Harold smiled wryly. "It's not that old SEAL-Beret rivalry which makes you say that, is it, Captain?"

"Rivalry! The idea of a SEAL being jealous of a G.B. is about as ridiculous as . . . Dolly Parton being jealous of Twiggy!"

My older friend and adviser laughed out loud. "Well, as long as you don't feel strongly about it. Okay, Captain, you know where to pick up your equipment. I've given you another Farallon-

Oceanic underwater propulsion vehicle—try to take better care of this one. And good luck. See you in a week or two.''

As I left the lab, I heard the steel firedoor close and lock behind me. Colonel D. Harold Westervelt had work to do . . .

9

Back at the docks, the fishing guides with morning half-day trips were already in, cleaning their fish. The charters stood around like proud old pros, getting their pictures taken with their catch of cuda, dolphin, wahoo, and billfish, while envious tourists looked on. Gulls circled overhead, squawking.

Man, you shoulda seen the damn shark we had on. . . .

Dang arms are still tired from that bull dolphin. . . .

Our captain seemed a little upset when my husband dropped the pole overboard, but I really don't think it was Joe's fault. . . .

Every day, twice a day, it's the Dead Fish and Tourist Show, live from Garrison Bight and Charterboat Row. I sat in *Sniper*'s port fighting chair, stern deck facing the pier, watching. There was a cold beer in my hand, and the sun felt good on my face, reflecting up off the green harbor water. Two boats down, an old friend, Captain Nels

Chester, stood hunched over the cleaning table steaking his catch while a middle-aged woman with a yellow straw hat bounced the same old tired questions off him. Every now and then he'd look over at me and wink.

"Yes, ma'am, twelve dolphin an' a coupla cuda is considered a pretty good catch."

"No, ma'am, I can't give you a partial refund."

"Yes, ma'am, you can buy fish at the market for five dollars a pound, but you can't *catch* 'em for five dollars a pound . . ."

You get too many like that. They weigh the number of steaks or fillets against the price of the trip. They're the ones who care nothing for the sport, who feel nothing in the fight of the fish; they're the ones who want only snapshots to show the folks back home, and enough dead meat to pay for the cost of the trip. I finished my beer and went up to the cleaning table to give Nels some verbal support. When the lady with the yellow straw hat felt my shadow cover her, she turned around.

"Did you catch *all* them fish, ma'am?" I had on my best gawking smile, loose-limbed, the big, harmless, and not-too-smart admirer.

"Well, yes . . . ah . . . my husband and I caught them. But I was just telling the captain here that I don't feel the number of fish we caught justifies the rather extravagant rates—"

I cut her off, looking at Nels. "Captain Chester, how do you do it? Why is it you're the one to always catch all the fish?"

Nels looked down at the table, fighting back the

laughter. "Jus' lucky, I guess, Captain MacMorgan. 'Course, I had a coupla real good fishermen with me, too."

That made the lady straighten. "Why, thank you!" She looked at the row of fish again, the dolphin now a faded yellow in death. "I guess there are more there than I thought."

She went off flushed with pleasure to find her husband, thanking Nels and promising to call him the next time they were in Key West. When she was out of earshot, Nels let it go, a big rolling burst of laughter. "Jesus criminy, MacMorgan, you ought to go on the stage, an' that's no shit."

"Seems I can remember you helping me out a time or two."

"Sure, sure, but the way you handled that woman . . . ha!"

"Two real good fishermen, huh?"

"Yeah, I guess I was doin' it too. That lady there couldn't catch her ass with a grappling hook, an' that's a natural fact. If they ever do come back, I hope she forgets my number."

Back in the salon, I turned the little fan so that it would sweep across me as I sat in the pilot's chair. I had another beer, Copenhagen wry against lower lip, and the little folder D. Harold Westervelt had given me. I went over the list of commercial fishermen who regularly worked the area. I checked off the ones I knew to be honest and dependable, and made a short list of those I didn't know. I'd call their names in to Norm Fizer and have his people do a more complete bio on each. There were three groups of treasure hunters with state permits to search and salvage around the Marquesas. I knew one of the guys, Buster Ronstadz, a big tough customer who had been arrested more than once in Key West for drunk and disorderly. Buster was a good example of the treasure-hunter type: he'd failed at just about everything else—commercial fishing, dive-shop operator, fishing guide—and hunting Spanish gold seemed to be part of the natural progression toward his own ruin. Buster was the loudmouthed bully type, and I'd heard something recently about him. What? And then I remembered: his wife had been hospitalized with a few broken ribs, claiming to have fallen down the steps—an odd excuse when a police investigation showed her to live in a single-story mobile home. I made a little star by Buster's name. He was one to watch.

There was a lengthy report on the team of Cuban-American treasure hunters. There were dozens of them, with a confusing host of surnames. All had one thing in common: each belonged to a fairly small organization called the Council of Liberty, a Miami-based organization which, in the minds of some, at least, had rather dubious motives. A note at the bottom of the report read:

''The Council of Liberty is presently under investigation. At least one, and possibly more, of the Cuban-American organizations in Miami secretly believes it to be a pro-Castro agency. As of yet, however, their claims are completely unsubstantiated. The Council is known to have financed and manned private military maneuvers in the Everglades, training, ostensibly, for the common

Cuban-American goal to oust Castro and retake
Cuba by force. Our investigation is expected to be
complete by the end of this year.''

I took a sip of beer and sighed. Great. Just great.
They could tell me everything I needed to know—
in three months.

The last report was on Jason Boone's group. It
was impressive, to say the least. War hero, brilliant student of archaeology and history at the
University of Iowa, and founder of a highly re-
garded religious organization called Christ's Children of America. His group had raised nearly a
million dollars to help feed, clothe, and educate
the poverty-stricken in Appalachia, and had sent
missionary teams to Europe, of all places. Reading
the report, I felt rather small and meek in the
swath Jason Boone had cut in his short lifetime.
He was one of the good ones; one of America's
straight-arrows who apparently had been broken
by all the needless death and suffering he saw in
Vietnam. But he had regrouped quickly and found
his way. I knew how it could happen. In Nam
there were only three ways to escape the hell:
drugs, death, or God. He had made the most sensible choice. In my long early years there, I just
rode with the hell, and tempered the horror with
an awesome amount of beer. I found the knowledge that he would be somewhere in the Marquesas area with me strangely reassuring—not
because he was a man of God (I think even less
about religion than I do about geometry) but because he was, at least, someone to turn to. Not
even the Navy personnel who later would help
me load my gear knew what I would be doing.

And the open sea beyond the Marquesas is one hell of a lot of emptiness.

I got a notebook and scribbled down the port addresses of the Cuban-American group and of Buster Ronstadz. If I was going out to watch the Cuban shrimp boat, I might as well do a little amateur sleuthing and see if I could find out what had happened to Gifford Remus—and his treasure.

It was one of those tacky little trailer parks at the edge of town: a domino series of bleached paint and aluminum life-sized cartons raised on concrete blocks. Dirt yards, broken children's toys on the ground, ragged, halfhearted attempts at landscaping with a few bright flowers and citrus trees—all of which looked as haggard as stray cats. There's an air of despair about these places. An atmosphere of too many pointless comings and goings. The cars in the dirt drives looked as broken-down and uncared-for as the trailers, and bored, haunted faces peered out at me as I whistled my way toward Lot # 13, the Ronstadz residence. It was soap-opera time, and I could hear dim organ music coming from a dozen separate televisions. *Edge of Darkness, As the World Turns*—escapes for the abandoned trailer women, contrived dramas for the lonely. Dry wash fluttered on a rope strung between trees in the stillness.

"Who's there?"

The thin face of a woman in her early thirties peered out at me through a crack as wide as the chain lock would allow.

"My name's MacMorgan, Mrs. Ronstadz. Dusky MacMorgan."

"If it's about the washer, we sent our payment in yesterday. You'll get your money. Sent it straight to the main office at Sears."

"It's not about the washer, Mrs. Ronstadz. I came to see your husband."

A cigarette hung from her thin lips. It swung up and down as she spoke. "My husband ain't here. Don't know when he's coming back."

"It's pretty important, Mrs. Ronstadz."

I could feel it coming. Strangers scare the lonely. She was going to slam the door in my face. So I made my move. You have to play these things by ear, right or wrong. I pulled the gold chain from my pocket and held it up in the bright October sunlight. "It's about this," I said.

I saw the intake of breath, the burning eyes.

"If that's my husband's, I'll just take it off your hands right now."

"It's not your husband's. If I could just come in for a moment?"

She slid the chain and opened the door wide. "Sure. But, like I said, he ain't home right now."

It was one of those trailers that remind you of a giant matchbox. Dingy yellows and rounded porcelain edges on the small refrigerator and stove. Grease had coagulated on the plywood cupboards, and there was the dank odor of fried eggs, roach spray, and cigarette smoke. She lighted another Winston, exhaling through her nose. "So why do you want to talk to Buster if that chain ain't his?"

"Because I know where to find more of these but I might need some help to do it."

"Might need some help, or do need some help?"

I shrugged. "Might. I don't know too much about treasure hunting. I heard your husband does."

She gave me a long look of appraisal. She wore a mouse-colored sack dress. She was tall, thin, brown-haired, and her breasts sagged braless beneath the material. She motioned me toward a chair in the narrow living room, switched off the TV set, then took a seat herself, holding her ribs painfully.

"I can't speak for Buster, but I think he'll be interested. He ain't been doing too good out there." And then, almost to herself, she added, "He ain't been doing too good at anything, lately."

"So when can I talk to him? Is he out in his boat?"

She shook her head. "Naw, he got back in yesterday. Had to get supplies."

"How long was he out?"

"Two weeks. But he says he found—" She cut herself off.

"Found what?"

She got up, searched for matches, lit another cigarette. "You better talk to Buster, mister." She looked at me again. "Say, ain't I seen you someplace? You look like this guy I saw in a movie once."

"No, not me." I smiled at her. "I'm just a fishing guide. Tell Buster my name and he'll know where to find me."

She brushed the hair out of her face, suddenly concerned with her appearance. She checked the clock on the wall. "Well, he ain't gonna be back all afternoon. Out getting drunk, I suppose." She came closer, eyes brighter. "You're welcome to wait here, mister. I got some beer in the fridge. I get so goddam bored here, it would be a pleasure to have someone to . . . talk to." It was the sadly common invitation. We were alone, a mature man, a mature woman, in the lonely little house with the husband away. I wondered in how many towns and houses and trailer parks across the nation the same game was being played at that very moment. In our fast-paced existence of interstate highways and business trips on jet planes, we have all become victims. I watched her nipples rise beneath the thin material and her eyes grow bright, and I knew. Our mobility has served only to emphasize our loneliness and to heighten our awareness of the universal void, and so we grasp at the quick intimacy of sex as if it would slow our warp-speed journey toward death. I felt sorry for her. Buster Ronstadz was no prince. And this trailer was no castle. Life for Mrs. Ronstadz hadn't turned out as neatly as it did on her TV programs. And it was slipping away from her all too quickly.

I stood up. She put her hand on my chest, tracing the line of buttons toward my pants. "Honest. He's not gonna be back for a couple more hours."

I was willing to play the verbal game, to spare her any rejection she couldn't rationalize. But nothing more.

"Geez, I'd like to. I really would." I checked my

watch. "But I have this damn meeting. Just tell your husband I'll see him around."

She took a step back and smiled. "Ain't that the way it always goes? People so busy they ain't got time for the good things. Well . . . Buster don't spend too much time here and . . . well, you know where to find me."

As I left, the wind caught the aluminum door and it slammed behind me. I heard an infant squawl, and heard Mrs. Ronstadz scream for it to shut up. Good luck on your journey, lady. You'll need it.

I called the marina where the Cuban-American group was supposed to stay when they were in port. Like Buster Ronstadz, I wanted to let them know I would be out there, and let them think I knew where Gifford Remus had found his treasure. If they were interested enough and ruthless enough, they would make a move on me. And I would be ready and waiting. I talked to a dockmaster with a sour disposition. No, they weren't back in from the Marquesas; no, he didn't know when they'd be back in, and there were too many goddam Cubans on the island as it was, and he didn't give a shit if they ever came back. Nice guy. I got another quarter from my pocket and tried Rigaberto Herrera at the office, then at his home.

"Dusky? Hey—you just caught me. Just getting ready to go out and run with my wife. Do me a favor, *amigo,* and tell me you have to see me right away. My wife will believe that—get me out of this damn torture for tonight at least."

I could hear his wife laughing in the back-ground. "Sorry, buddy. Just wanted to see if you'd found out anything more about Gifford Remus."

"Naw, not a thing. Coast Guard didn't find a sign of his tent—just the remains of his fire. And somebody had tried to hide that. Still no body. We figure he drowned, and someone going by saw an unattended camp and stole what was worth stealing."

"Do you believe that, Rigaberto?"

"About as much as you do. Why would a thief try to hide a campfire?"

"So what are you going to do about it?"

"Dusky, in the past three weeks we've had seven fatalities or near fatalities from bad drugs. Teenagers, Dusky—one girl was twelve years old. Another kid went nuts on some kind of angel-dust crap and stabbed his baby brother. When I get done running that down, and maybe working on the other dozen or so unsolved murders we have on the books, *then* I might have time to work on the Remus case. You understand?"

"I'm sorry, Rigaberto. I know how pressed you are. But look, I'm going out to the Marquesas to-morrow afternoon to do a little fishing. I'll keep an eye open for you, and if you hear anything more, maybe you could give me a call on VHF 16?"

"Fishing, huh?"

"I'm taking my poles. Honest."

"Why do you lie to an old friend like this?"

"Because it's easier than the truth."

He sighed. "Just don't kill anybody, Dusky. I'm busy enough as it is."

By the time I got back to my boat with enough canned goods, beer, and food to last three men for two weeks, it was nearing sunset. The charterboats were all in, washed down and secured, and Nels Chester sat in one of his fighting chairs with a beer. Cool of the evening, and people walked the docks, some hand in hand. Ibis flew in white formation against the orange sphere that settled itself over the western horizon of Key West, and the channel markers came on flashing red or white, every four slow seconds.

"Set a spell, Dusky."

I put the box of supplies in the cabin, got a cold Hatuey from the little refrigerator, went back outside, and took a seat beside Nels. It was good sitting there watching the orange light melt into the darkness of the island; a good time for fish stories and friendly laughter. So much had changed, so much had happened, but there was still this.

"You want to walk on down to Stevie's houseboat? Sounds like he's throwin' a little party down there. Heard there's a convention of Chicago secretaries in town who get the giggles around fishing guides with southern accents. How's 'bout it?"

Sure. Why not. Drink a few beers, exchange a few stories with friends. It wouldn't hurt to go out and relax before heading to the Marquesas.

I relaxed all right.

I almost relaxed myself to death.

Stevie Wise's *Fred Astaire* is a forty-six-foot floating bachelor pad with an interesting history. It
had been owned by some northern insurance
salesman who had an impressive string of mis-
tresses, all of whom had, at one time or another,
made the boat their wayward home. To keep his
women happy, the insurance salesman had
equipped it with a massive circular bed in the
master stateroom, added a hugh bathtub, and
moodied up the lounge area with an erotic
mural—suggestive enough to be both confusing
and shocking—which covered a whole wall. When
the insurance salesman's wife found out the boat
was sold by the divorce courts to more business-
minded people—drug runners. The drug runners
abused the furniture, ruined the engine, and got
busted by the feds. Stevie likes to point to the
bullet holes in the forward bulkhead and tell how
the jealous husband of a famous movie star almost
got him. He's lying, of course. He's also lying
when he promises to someday take the pretty girl

he happens to be with on a long cruise. With a bottom hopelessly fouled and no engine, it would take a tugboat to budge the *Fred Astaire.*

The party was already in full swing by the time Nels and I got there. They were on the third keg of beer, and had sent a team to go for more. I recognized a lot of the people there, mostly charterboat people and commercial fishermen. But there were also a few outsiders. Stevie came up with mugs of beer for us, smiling broadly.

"Showed four girls the stateroom tonight! *Four.*" He wiped his brow as if he had just finished digging a ditch. "Dusky, I'm so tired I just pray I don't get another chance." At that very moment, a pretty dark-haired woman with stern-looking glasses came and took him by the arm and led him away.

"And where's that funny round bed of yours I've heard so much about . . ." she was saying as they disappeared down the corridor.

It had been too long since I had talked with old friends and laughed, really laughed. No matter what happens, no matter what horrors we encounter, most of us go on living, and the laughter goes on shielding us from the certainty of death. The few secretaries who had not already found a fishing guide to make their vacation memorable stood in a little cluster in the lounge, giggling, tilting their heads, studying the mural on the wall. They kept eyeing us: a half-dozen sunburned city women, most in their mid-twenties. Finally, the two prettiest came over to Nels and me.

"What exactly *are* those people doing in that painting?"

They had obviously made their selections. The one standing by me had long blond hair that was carefully styled to fall over one brown eye. The Bacall look. And with her fine, angular face, it wasn't a bad try. She wore expensive jogging shorts and a loose open blouse that displayed a burnt-orange swimsuit and the thin but ripe body beneath. Nels's girl was doing the talking. She had a pixie haircut and a face to match.

"We've been studying it and studying it, and we just can't figure out what the artist had in mind."

Nels winked at me and grinned. "Ladies, let's just say if them folks was lamp cords, every part of their bodies would be glowin'."

"What? Oh!" The pixie broke into loud laughter. Mine barely smiled. "Don't you get it, Fayette? Look at it real close and you can see that they're . . ." She broke into laughter again, blushing and slapping at Nels. "I never saw anything like that in Chicago!"

Nels swept her away toward the aft deck, leaving me uncomfortably alone with the blond, Fayette. She toyed with her drink, her head swinging back and forth as if she were looking for a cab. Someone turned the record player up even farther and the whole houseboat seemed to vibrate.

"It doesn't agree with your taste in art?"

"Hmm . . . ? Oh." She smiled thinly. "Hardly."

"First time in Key West?"

"Yes."

"How do you like it?"

"I don't."

"Have you noticed how those of us who work around boats smell of fish?"

She gave me an odd look. "As a matter of fact . . ."

"Lady," I said, "you're the one who approached us with that stupid question about the mural."

"It wasn't my idea, believe me."

"And I'm no more interested in charming that dandy little body of yours into bed than you are. I was just trying to make conversation, lady. Nothing more."

I turned and moved carefully through the party crowd, outside. It was a nice night: silken mist of autumn stars, and the moon threw a white path across the harbor. And I had just refilled my mug from the tap and leaned against the railing, enjoying the view, when I felt someone touch my shoulder. It was the blond.

She shook her head as if embarrassed, then stuck out her hand. "My name is Fayette Kunkle. Willing to start fresh?"

I took her hand—nice hand, dry and firm. "MacMorgan," I said. "Dusky MacMorgan. And of course I am."

She leaned against the rail beside me. "I'm sorry about being so . . . short in there."

"Don't worry about it. I've actually been grumpy myself."

"Oh, it's not that. Well, maybe I am a little grumpy, but there's a reason."

She thought for a moment. "I'm afraid it's the way my friends are acting in there. They're really not like that, they aren't. In our group are some of the finest legal secretaries in Chicago. They have husbands, some of them even have children. But ever since we came down here for the convention, they've been running around like boy-crazy teenagers."

"Well, Miss Kunkle, I guess it's only natural for those of us without halos to occasionally act human."

"I'm doing it again?"

"Maybe." I laughed. "You're getting this from an expert, you know. I'm saddled with the malady of self-righteousness myself. And then I see a kindred spirit and realize what a big pain in the ass I must be."

"Pain in the ass, am I!" She grinned when she said it.

"Yes."

"And do you mind telling me why . . . MacMorgan, was it?"

"Because you judge without sympathy. Not that you, or I or anybody else, for that matter, is qualified to judge the actions of another human being. But if you're going to do it, you ought to throw in a little understanding for good measure."

"So now I'm not just a pain in the ass, but I'm also an unsympathetic pain in the ass?"

"You're getting this from the horse's mouth, Fayette. Don't forget. Okay, so your friends who are upstanding women and wives and mothers in Chicago come to Key West and let their hair down. You can spend a lifetime with one person and never know what her most private hopes and needs are. After they've dropped some daydream ballast down here, they'll probably go back home and carry on their stable business and family lives. I'm not saying it's right, I'm just saying, who are pains in the ass like you and me to judge?" I took a sip of beer. "And I haven't talked this much in a year."

She told me about herself. She looked about twenty-two and had a nice voice, soft and low amid the insulated din of the party going on within. At first she stuck to the impersonal things: job, education, her childhood in Columbus. She was the daughter of a Lutheran minister, they'd had a real smart collie named Lassie, and her mother was just the best, best cook ever. She had attended Northwestern University on an academic scholarship, and the only reason she was working as a secretary was so that she could go back to school and get a law degree. There had been the usual bad marriage to her high school sweetheart, and now some new involvement. She talked around it, waiting for me to draw her out. But finally she took it up herself. It was a Chicago physician. A brilliant man. And she was in love with him; madly, passionately in love. She had been seeing him for two years. But there was one problem. He was married.

"And you were disappointed in your friends?" I asked. It was a mistake. I saw her eyes narrow and her nostrils flare.

"Now who's being the high-moraled pain in the ass?" For a second I thought she was going to slap me. "I love him, Dusky. And he loves me."

"But he loves his wife, too."

She nodded. It was a story made trite by millions, but unique because she was involved. She

kept asking how it could have happened, and why
it happened, and why couldn't she just damn well
give him up. At the prodding of her friends, she
had agreed to come to Key West to get away, to
think things over. She went to the island bars, and
the island parties, all of which served only to
make her more depressed and confused.

"It's as if I'm just waiting for another man, another good man, to come along and sweep me off
my feet." She caught my eyes when she said it,
and was immediately embarrassed. "I didn't mean
to imply . . ."

"Forget it," I said. "I meant what I told you in
there. I'm not interested—and not because you
aren't attractive and intelligent. I'm just not."

She toyed with her drink. "You're married."

"I was."

"Divorced?"

"No."

She started to ask the obvious next question,
then reconsidered. Smart woman. "It really is a
pretty night, isn't it, Dusky?" She brushed her
blond hair off her face and leaned out over the
water looking at her own reflection. "Isn't this
hairdo awful? My friends talked me into this, too.
Vacation, a new look—but a new life doesn't always follow, does it?"

I said nothing.

"Dusky, would it be proper for a woman to ask
a new male friend to take her for a walk?"

"Absolutely. Let's go."

We walked up past the marina, away from the
smoke and the noise of the *Fred Astaire*. She took
fast, long strides—city strides. Hurry, hurry, slip

down the sidewalks through the mass of flesh and strange humanity. But she wasn't in Chicago, and I had to keep reminding her to slow down. We stood on the little cement sweep of causeway which stretches over Garrison Bight. I told her what the different night markers and range lights meant. By then, there was a pleasant understanding between us made uneasy by a musky sexuality. I turned once and felt my arm brush the abundant thrust of breasts. She shuddered, exhaling.

"Well!"

"Well . . ."

I checked my watch. "I guess I'd better be getting back to my boat. Got to get some sleep and it's after midnight."

"That late?"

"Uh-huh. Going on a little trip tomorrow."

"When will you be back?" She said it too fast, running all her words together, and we both laughed.

"A week. Maybe two."

"Hummm. We've got three more days here. I don't suppose you ever get up to Chicago?"

"Almost never."

We walked back in silence. When we were about a hundred yards from my boat, she started to say something. I knew what it was because I had been thinking the same thing. But she never got it out. There was something wrong aboard *Sniper*. At first I didn't know what. Too much beer, probably. But then I realized—there was a light coming from the starboard port. And I had left only the salon light on.

II

I walked stealthily along the cement pier—
ridiculous, really, to try to be quiet when music
from the *Fred Astaire* blasted all across the midnight harbor. I had told Fayette to stay where she
was and walked away from her questioning look.
There was a light on all right, and I saw the silhouette of a man cross the little oblong hatch.
Strange shape to the face. I got closer, looking in,
and understood why. He was wearing a ski mask,
making a methodical search of my forward berth.
I reached for my little Gerber fishing knife, but it
wasn't there. I'd taken it off when I had gone to
see Mrs. Ronstadz. And hadn't thought to put it
back on.

That's what happens when you let your guard
down.

That's what happens when you relax. Too much
beer, too much relaxing, too stupid.

I watched him from the window. He found the
Russian assault rifle I had hidden beneath the mattress of the port bunk. He picked it up as if he

knew how to use it—then put it back just the way he had found it. That told me all I wanted to know. Any common thief would have taken it. This guy was after something special, and I knew just what it was. I touched the weight of the Spanish gold chain in my pocket. He'd have to kill me to get it.

Quietly, I moved back toward the stern deck, along the finger of pier. I had a plan. There was a shark billy stashed beneath the port rodholder. I'd get it, soften the guy's skull a bit, then make him talk. I had a feeling he could tell me an interesting story or two about the strange disappearance of a strange little man.

Carefully, I stepped over onto my boat. I didn't want any shift in trim to telegraph my approach. In the thin moonlight I found it. The club fit the curve of my hand perfectly. I had him now. I turned to find a hiding place in the shadows of the deck, and suddenly there was an arm across my chest, and the stiletto point of a knife pressed up against my Adam's apple.

I expected him to say something, to threaten me with some grim death threat. Instead, he gave an odd sort of low whistle, and my cabin door opened a moment later. The man with the ski mask I had been watching exited. He was a big rough-looking character, and from the strength with which the other one held me, he was just as big. The one in the ski mask approached me, holding a flashlight in my eyes so that I couldn't see. I felt his hands searching my pockets. Once they got the chain I knew I was a dead man. I had to make a move and make it quick. I relaxed; let my upper body muscles go limp. When you want someone to loosen their hold on you, the worst thing to do is struggle. I felt the arm around me slacken momentarily. It was the only chance I had. In the same swift motion, I kicked out with my right leg toward the groin area of ski mask, shoved back with my left leg, and drove my elbow as deeply as I could toward the bladder of the man with the knife. I felt the blade slice across my chin and up my cheek, and heard at the same time two loud groans. I'd hit my marks. I had hoped the impact of elbow on stomach would knock us both into the water. If I got him in the water he was a dead man, knife or no knife. But it didn't. I had no choice but to work on the man with the stiletto first. Keeled over in pain, he made a halfhearted thrust at my eyes when I came at him. I kicked the knife from his hand and, on the backstroke of my leg, caught him just behind the ear with my heel. It was a good shot, but not good enough. He was down but not out. I turned quickly to meet ski mask. But he just stood there. Calm, cool, seemingly unaffected by my kick to the groin. And then I knew why he was so self-assured when I saw what he was holding in his hands. It was a stubby blackness in the weak moonlight—a snub-nosed .38.

"Look," I said, "I know what you want. The chain. It's in my pocket."

"Get it," he said. Harsh voice, thick Southern accent.

I wiped the hot slick of blood from my face, took the chain from my pocket, and, without hesitating, tossed it overboard into the water.

I expected his head to turn when I threw it. I expected to kick the gun from his hand as his eyes followed the arcing gold fortune into the water. But his head didn't turn, his eyes never flinched.

He was good.

Too good.

And I knew I was a goner.

"Stupid bastard," he said. "Silly stupid bastard."

I heard the hammer click as he pulled it back. He leveled the gun at my nose. And then:

"Hold it! Police!"

It was a woman's voice, and it shocked me as much as it did him. The guy who'd had the knife was already on his feet, running. Ski mask hesitated, turned the gun on me again, then followed behind, jumping from the transom to the pier, escaping into the darkness of the parking lot. I hoped he would live to regret his decision.

It was Fayette Kunkle, the pretty woman with the odd name. Her eyes widened, horrified, and I realized what I must have looked like.

"Hey, I'm fine—really."

"Oh my God, Dusky, oh my God, what did they do to you?"

Her hands trembled as she hurried to pull blue makeup tissue from her purse. She was crying, scared out of her wits. "I've got to get you to the hospital; we've got to call the police."

I pulled her hands from my face. "We're going to do no such thing."

"But Dusky, your face . . . all this blood . . ." She stopped then as some awful suspicion came over her. "Wait a minute. No police . . . you aren't . . . aren't a criminal or something, are you?''

I took the few clean tissues she had and wiped her tears away, laughing. "No, lady, I'm no crook. You watch too many movies."

"You'd better be thankful I do. When I saw what was happening to you I almost screamed. Instead I did what the woman cops do on TV."

"You're right," I said. "I'm thankful. Damn thankful."

She followed me down into the little head behind the booth on the port side. I switched on the light and studied my face. I was a mess, all right. I looked like one of those bloodied animals on the covers of the pro wrestling magazines. It was a long slice, from cheek to the corner of my right eye. Close. All too close. It wouldn't need stitches, but it would add another scar to my collection. I poured alcohol onto a washcloth, flinching at the shock of it. "I want you to do something for me, Fayette."

"Anything, Dusky. But shouldn't we call the police? They could find out who those two men were and why they were—"

"I know why, and I know who. It was one nasty bastard by the name of Buster Ronstadz, and if you get me my mask and underwater flashlight out of that locker over there, I'll show you exactly what they were after."

She sighed. I could see her face plainly in the harsh mirror light. Soft brown eyes, pale glint of long blond hair, perfect skin beneath sunburn. "I'll get your things for you on two conditions."

"And they are?"

"First of all, you have to promise to let me bandage that cut. I know first aid, and that has to be taken care of properly."

"And the second?"

She averted her gaze, took up the washcloth and began dabbing at my face. Very businesslike. "Secondly," she said, "I don't . . . well, dammit, I don't want you to make me leave tonight."

"No."

"Please, Dusky. I don't know what your problem is, but something has hurt you and . . . we don't have to sleep together, we could just talk, and . . ."

She took a step back, surprised. "Look at me, will you! I've known you two hours and I'm already begging to spend the night with you!"

I reached out and touched her soft hair. "We'll talk it over," I said. "Later."

"Okay, Dusky. Later . . ."

The Key Wester Inn is one of the island's better motels. It's located on the south side, away from the fast-food traps, setting back in on its own little estate where Roosevelt Boulevard sweeps along the sea. Jason Boone had his people out on the early-morning lawn, eighteen of them sitting in a tight circle beneath a banyan tree. At first I thought it was just a group meeting. I leaned my old Schwinn bicycle against the curb and went ambling up, full of good cheer, face gauzed and taped and all. And when I got closer and realized it was no group strategy meeting at all, I felt like a complete fool. They were praying. I'd come up like a stray dog on a private Sunday-morning church service.

"And God, we ask that You aid us in our work and help us in our humble attempt to bring the lost back into Your guiding light . . ."

It was my young friend Wayne Peters who was leading the prayer. I was surprised. Back on my boat, he hadn't seemed the type. Like most of the other young men and women, he wore a white T-shirt and jeans. His shoulders stretched out into the sleeves of the T-shirt, and his big farm-boy biceps protruded. He looked up as he prayed, noticed me, and gave me a big funny wink.

"And protect us in our upcoming days at sea, and help those of us who must stay behind know that they also serve because there just isn't enough room . . ."

That got a giggle or two. Praying or not, the kid had a sense of humor.

As I watched, entertaining thoughts of trying to sneak away unseen, I felt someone come up beside me. It was Jason. He smiled, offered his hand, and mouthed the words, "Follow me."

We went down the little walkway beneath cool trees and the scent of jasmine, out into the big patio pool area. It was a large saltwater pool, coral-green, and enclosed by little shops, a bar, and a glassed-in restaurant. We took seats at one of the umbrellaed poolside tables. A waitress with an Australian accent was there immediately, and we both ordered coffee.

"Good to see you, Dusky. I'm sorry you didn't

get here earlier. You could have participated in our service."

"It was nice of you to send Wayne to invite me. He seems like a good kid."

Jason nodded, his big Viking head bobbing up and down. "They all are. Great kids. I love every one of them." He looked at me and smiled. "Should I ask about that bandage on your face?"

"It's a long story, and I expect we'll have plenty of time to talk out on the Marquesas. But first of all, were you serious when you offered to tell me some of the finer points of treasure hunting?"

"Certainly." The coffee came and we spent some comfortable moments doctoring it. Good coffee. "Dusky," he said, "I have two great loves in my life. My religion, and my work. As an archaeologist, I have this great horror of treasure hunters getting to the big wrecks before they can be properly charted and studied. So, in our short time here, I've made an attempt to work with the treasure hunters."

"Any luck?"

He grinned. "I'm afraid the treasure hunter is not a breed to be reasoned with. There are two other groups working in the Marquesas area—of course, you rarely ever see them or their boats, because there is so much water out there. But the most efficient of the two seems to be a group of Cuban-Americans. They're doing everything right: theodolite operators—kind of surveyors, really— stationed on towers to keep their magnetometer boat on course, the best equipment, and, it seemed to me, a very disciplined crew."

"And how did they seem when you approached them?"

"Cold at best. Their leader is a fellow named Emanuel Ortiz. Very aloof, very military-like. He didn't have time to discuss it."

"And the other group?"

"Poorly equipped and poorly managed. I'm surprised one of them hasn't been killed by now."

I thought it over. Should I lay a partial hand on the table? I decided to give it a shot. Some people you have to trust. "One of them almost was—last night. That's why I'm sipping coffee from the left side of my mouth this morning."

"But why you?"

So I told him the story. Most of the story, anyway. Gifford Remus, the gold chain, and the fight. I pulled the chain from my pocket and laid it on the table. I watched his face closely, I watched for greed and saw none—only delight.

"Dusky, this is beautiful . . . magnificent." He studied it anxiously. "Look at the workmanship in this—each link spiraled by hand. And you know, this wasn't just any piece of jewelry owned by a rich nobleman. Each link has a specific weight; forty-two links equaled one escudo. It's wonderful."

"I'll let you study it a little closer when . . . we're finished out there. But now it's a pretty dangerous trinket to have. I think Gifford Remus was murdered because of it."

Jason nodded. "Your friend Detective Herrera feels the same way."

"He told you that?"

"Not in so many words. In his own way, he

was warning me to be careful. He didn't have to. I knew as much after I made an attempt to talk to your late-night visitor . . . Ronstadz?"

"Yeah. Buster Ronstadz."

"He wouldn't even let my skiff land. He came out with a gun and threatened to shoot me if he ever caught me or any of my group in his 'area' again. He meant it, too. I know the look. He's big and he's brutal." He cleared his throat, suddenly nervous. "Dusky, I want to be honest with you. I didn't invite you out here just to give you information and see if you would cooperate with us. I'm afraid I know that you're more than just another treasure hunter—"

"What?"

"Your reputation precedes you, I'm afraid. I fought in the same war you did, and your exploits in the early days of Nam had become almost legendary by the time I got there. What did they call you— SEAL of Sherwood? Something like that because of what you could do with the Cobra crossbow?"

"That was a long time ago, Jason."

"After you left me at the Sheriff's Department and I finally realized who you were, I knew that you would know something about me that I can hardly even admit to myself."

"That you didn't have to kill that Abbey character, but you did anyway?"

I watched the words sting him. He wiped his face with a big copper-colored hand. "I was a Green Beret, Dusky. I was taught how to disarm a man, and I was also taught how to kill a man. When he came at me with that knife it was like I was back in the jungle again, and . . ."

"I know how it is, Jason. And believe me when I say this: you have nothing to feel guilty about, because it wasn't you who did the killing. It was the guy you wanted to leave back in Nam. But you can't ever truly leave him; nor can I, nor any of the rest of us. He'll always be there, deep inside."

He looked up and tried a weak smile. "Then you did know?"

"Not really. At first I thought you were some YMCA karate boob. Did you say something to Wayne about . . . me?"

"I'm afraid I did. The kids seem so fascinated by that sort of thing." His eyes grew glassy, haunted, hollow. "But they don't know the horror of it, do they? They don't know the awful, awful horror. And I wish to God I didn't."

As we stood to go to Jason's room to go over charts and the finer points of treasure hunting, his group came running by, dressed in swimsuits. I had never seen so many good-looking kids in my life. They looked like a Swedish gymnastics team at play.

"If the world was made up all of smart, dedicated, God-loving kids like that, there would have been no Vietnam," Jason said. He still had the haunted look that I knew so well. "Wouldn't it be nice if we never had to worry about war again . . ."

12

Funny the things you think about when you are alone at sea. At sunset on a Sunday I powered out of Garrison Bight, steering from the flybridge of *Sniper*, headed for the Marquesas. I moved past the soft feathered rows of Australian pines and coconut palms leaning in windward strands, past the old submarine base at Truman Annex, past the squat dun hulk of Fort Zachary Taylor, and picked up the first black-and-white nun buoy marking Southwest Channel. It rocked and weaved in the turquoise wake of my twin 453 GMC diesels. Key West dropped behind: white beach glowing like gold in the tawny sunset light, the radio beacon, and, finally, the red-and-white-checkered water tower, which is the first thing you raise when approaching that old pirate island. It felt good to be at sea again. Alone. Lee Johnson and I had had a nice trip; a sweet sort of healing time for both of us. But when we had finally parted, when she had finally stepped off *Sniper* and waved goodbye, I had felt my sadness tem-

pered with relief. It was the same sort of relief I
had felt back when I was young and dating. The
first thing I wanted to do after dropping the girl
off was stop in some shadowed darkness a block
away to fart, urinate, and take a dip of snuff. To
revel in my independence, to relax in the comfort
of my own company. I thought about these things
as I steered from the flybridge. Funny things,
strange things. The sun boiled above the far sea,
then was absorbed by it: orange and silver and
hues of red coating my westerly course for the
Marquesas. The wind had swung around out of
the north. Not wind really; a cool night breeze.
But on the water of the Florida Straits, it doesn't
pay to take chances. So I ran the Southwest Channel course, in the thin lee.

I had felt the same sort of relief, too, that morning after saying my goodbyes to Fayette Kunkle.

Some woman.

Some lover.

I felt something low in my stomach stir as I
remembered how it had been.

The *Sniper*'s cabin is close quarters indeed for a
healthy woman and a big healthy man. She had
made coffee. We talked. It was warm in the cabin,
so she took off the loose shirt she wore, covered
only by the burnt-orange swimsuit. She had done
a professional job of bandaging my knife wound.
I had sat meekly in the booth while she bent over
me. I watched a bead of sweat roll down her chest
and disappear into the ample cleavage of swimsuit. In the outline of thin material, I could see
what her breasts would look like: round, heavy;
sharp upward thrust of coned nipples.

"Dusky, you're trembling! Maybe I should get you to a hospital . . ."

"I don't think the doctors have a cure for the reason I'm shaking."

I had watched her step back and pretend not to realize what I was saying. But she knew. She was trembling herself.

"I think you'd better leave, Fayette . . ."

"No!"

"Fayette, I think it would be best."

She had come over to me clicking her tongue like an old maid.

"Look at what a mess your shirt is. It's ruined. Stand up and let me take it off."

So I had stood up dutifully and watched her face for the change of expression when she saw the shark scar. It's startling, to say the least. It's a wide full moon of raked, scarred flesh that circles across my side and disappears into my pants. She was shocked, speechless, embarrassed—and then I realized why.

"Fayette, this is not why I want you to leave. The shark cut me—but he didn't . . . ah . . . take anything."

"Oh God," she said, half laughing, half crying. "For a moment I felt like such an idiot. I thought . . . the direction that awful scar goes . . ."

I had pulled her close to me. "I know what you thought, but I really do think you ought to—"

She shushed me with a kiss. And another. And still another: openmouthed, soft lips. "You're hurt. I'll give the orders—just one self-righteous pain in the ass to another. There's a tie string on the back of this swimsuit . . ."

"I noticed . . ."

"Pull it . . ."

Fayette Kunkle was one of the fiery ones. Her cool demeanor fell away with our clothes. She was so thin the frame of ribs moved enticingly toward the full round veeing of hips and body hair, and her breasts were as I had imagined. Once the guard was down, there was no shyness in this one; nothing she would not do to please me; nothing I could not do to please her. In the feverish sweat of joining and touching, in the tangled maneuvers of love and the slow rock of the boat, we met as one again and again, then went beyond in the coupling which is the most tangible link of all humanity and all times.

"You really have to leave this morning?"

"Yes."

"Strange. So strange. I would never have thought that after only a few hours with another person, I could . . ."

"Your physician friend is a lucky man."

"Yes, in a way—because now I have discovered something very important about myself . . ."

The mind takes odd paths when you are alone at sea. I stood on the flybridge smiling, remembering, going over certain kind moments again and again. The dusk sea breeze was soft on the right side of my face, a bit of loose tape and gauze fluttering in the light wind. I went below and pulled my Marquesas chart out of the rack. I would be there in little more than an hour. I got the straightedge, found a good safe course, then adjusted the dial of the little Benmar autopilot and engaged it. The soft hydraulic whir of electronics took control of *Sniper* while I worked. I had had the running lights on: red and green haze of port and starboard bow lights and the soft white glow of stern light beneath the softer light of moon and stars over the black sea. I flicked on the Si-Tex radar system, hearing the rhythmic hum of the whirling antenna mounted above and forward. I watched for lime-green bleeps on the twelve-inch screen. None. Good clear sea, safe water. I punched off the running lights, cruising in darkness. The *Sniper* was built for darkness. And so was I.

At night, alone, you fiddle with things. You fart around and tinker, studying charts, and relax in the comfortable lift and heave of seas. I put coffee on to boil, and it filled the cabin with its good smell. Waiting, I got a cold beer and drank it slowly, enjoying it. I switched on the cabin light and sat in the booth with my chart—checking, occasionally, the sweep of radar screen, and standing to scan the darkness with my own eyes. Just in case. I got out Norm Fizer's folders, and matched the Loran coordinates of my search area with those on my chart. My area began a few degrees off the intersecting of the 43780 and 13876 lines, and went on to include about three square miles of water. One hell of a lot of sea. With the straightedge I squared the area with a pencil and realized that it wasn't the safest water around—it included most of the old bombing and strafing area. At the bottom of the folder was a scribbled note from Stormin' Norman: "Only permit available—be careful, you old fool!"

Thank God I wasn't really going to be looking for treasure.

I took the coordinates of my destination and, just for the hell of it, pushed the memory-lock buttons and punched in the figures, and the red digital glow of the Loran C flashed an estimated time of arrival at me and, by the way, you're .3 degree off course, buddy! You get hooked on electronics and, snakelike, they end up taking control of you.

"Screw you," I said out loud, grinning foolishly. "I *want* to be point-three degrees off course."

We lose a little something with every advancement, you know. We spend so much time crapping into flush toilets that we've forgotten that it's possible to live without plumbing. We spend so much time in cars that we've lost the joy of walking. But the little losses can turn deadly at sea. What happens when the electronics go out, and you've forgotten—or never learned—to read the stars, or the smell of the wind?

Odd, rambling thoughts at sea. In a boat. Alone. In a surge of independence, I poured myself a big mug of coffee, added a teaspoon of honey, then switched off all the electronics and climbed back up to the flybridge to take control.

Sitting in the rolling darkness and the sweet sync of muffled engines, I checked the green glow of Rolex. Thirty more minutes? It didn't matter.

I would anchor near the same reef where Lee Johnson and I had encountered the huge mako. There were plenty of fish there. And lobster. In the morning I would treat myself to espresso. Then I'd slip over and spear a nice fish for breakfast.

Grouper?

Naw, a nice snapper. Mutton snapper and fry it in thin strips with lime.

Wait a minute, MacMorgan! I caught myself. This was no vacation. This was going to be no two weeks of sun and fun, cold beer and fishing.

You've had your rest, dammit!

One strange little man is dead, and if it hadn't been for the woman you'd be faceup in the city morgue right now. You've got a score to settle with one big ugly bastard named Ronstadz, and you've got to keep tabs on that boat from Castro's commie nest just ninety miles to the south. And they've been having a tough time of it down there lately. Little bugs got to most of the sugarcane. And the fungus killed their precious tobacco crop. They've had whole neighborhoods fighting over windfall mangos. They're poor and they're godless and they're desperate.

And desperate people can be very, very deadly . . .

The little chain of Marquesas Keys finally came into dim view. First the distant, pulsing haze of the far corona of channel markers north of Crawfish Key. Then the shadowed flats of Man Key and Ballast Key.

Then the currented chop of Boca Grande Channel. More open water. Then a hint of gray outlines; the foggy grace of Gull Key and Mooney Harbor Key—and the encircling darkness of the Marquesas.

I ran along West Channel until I picked up the red flash of Cosgrove Shoal light, then powered north, 350 degrees. It was a still night. Lightning flared somewhere over the Tortugas. Silence and steady pulse of engines. Distant *awk-wawk* of a roosting bird from the low mangrove islands.

I studied the darkness around me for anchor lights and saw just one: faint, singular glow on the open sea. The sweeping green *bleep-bleep* of radar told me there were three others: one about four miles to the west-southwest; another to the west by northwest; another six miles out where the ocean had no bottom—the Cubans. I nosed *Sniper* safely wide of the three-foot shoal area, dropped the hook in about eleven feet of water near the reef, then shoved her astern, playing out plenty of scope. When I had eighty feet of line out, I stopped my sternway with a forward thrust, then trotted forward to snub her off.

The engines *ticked-ticked* with heat from the long trip.

The storm over the Tortugas had brought a coolness to the tropical autumn night, and swung the wind to the west. I went to the aft deck and checked the little Whaler I had tethered along behind. She was fine. It was still early: nine P.M. And there was work to do. With dividers, I transferred the grid of the radar screen to my chart. Then, as closely as I could, I made little penciled crosses where my four neighbors were anchored. It was exacting work, and my eyes hurt by the time I was finished.

It was beer time.

Time to relax.

I got the 4/0 Penn reel on its stubby boat rod, baited it with a catfish tail, and secured it in the holder. It was all of five minutes before I got my first strike: a sizzling run of fifty yards capped by a spectacular jump. There was phosphorescence in the water, and the fish splashed back down in a spray of green fire.

Tarpon. A late school of big ones.

They would help me wait . . .

13

I spent a long morning playing treasure hunter. It's work: hard, boring, and hot. But I knew that mine wasn't the only boat out there with radar, and someone could very easily be monitoring my activities.

I was supposed to be hunting for treasure.

So I played the game.

The "magnetometer" D. Harold Westervelt had requisitioned for me was cone-shaped, had a bright new coat of yellow paint over the original drab military green, and weighed a compact fifty pounds. It was built to home in on any underwater electronic devices within a hundred-yard radius. With it was a hand-sized beeper that would signal me of a find. Easy enough. The other treasure hunters would be towing real magnetometers—underwater metal detectors on which all the hopes and dreams of their owners were pegged. They were hunting gold and silver.

I was hunting one or more of them.

Hand over hand, I played out about fifty yards

of woven nylon line as the *Sniper* idled north across the sand flats. The Marquesas were cool green shapes to starboard, and the magnetometer dipped and dove astern on its line, then finally stayed down, running about three feet beneath the water, throwing its own wake. I watched closely to make sure it would not foul on the little Whaler, then went forward and gunned the engines up to 800 rpm. I had no theodolite operator on a tower to keep me on perfect course, so used the only thing I had—the Loran C in sync with the Benmar autopilot. If you run even a few points off course for more than a minute you can miss a chunk of sea bottom big enough to hold the base of the Empire State Building. And that's why I had never been interested in treasure hunting. Sure, it sounds romantic. But the chances of finding the minuscule bit of bottom which holds treasure even in a relatively small area—not to mention the whole damn sea—is so unlikely as to be ridiculous. Still, a few had done it. One or two by sheer luck. The rest by dedicating their lives.

I grabbed my aviator polaroids and the Bushnell zoom scope, put a bottle of beer in a cooler cup, then went up to the flybridge.

Run north three miles. Square it off. Run back three miles. Square it off and reset course. Up three miles, back three miles.

Boring, boring, boring . . .

Through the scope, I could see the Cuban shrimp boat plainly. Tiny black script on the stern, but I couldn't decipher the words.

They had come into the relative shallows off Marquesas Rock to anchor for the day. It was a great white vessel, outriggers folded like pterodactyl wings, with an upswept bow. It sat on the flat shimmer of sea caught in its own stillness.

Nothing stirred aboard.

Not unusual for a shrimp boat, really. Shrimpers work at night and sleep during the day. But they sure as hell weren't dragging in three-hundred feet of water. So what were they doing?

I'd give it a day, maybe, then work my way closer to them. Nothing obvious. Just a gold-hungry treasure hunter a little off course.

I sat on the flybridge amid the steady hum of engines, thinking. I thought about Gifford Remus and the conversation I'd had with him.

Strange little guy with his tale of ghosts and spirits. What had he said?

Hurricane. September 1622. The *Gaspar* foundered this way and struck the reef, then broke apart. "Ain't no real secret what reef they hit, Dusky, and folks has been lookin' for that treasure for a long time. But I'm the only one to figure out why nobody's found the main lode. Even with all their fancy gear, I'm the only one to figure it out! It's all right out—"

I swore at myself for not allowing him to finish.

It's all right out where, Gifford?

Where?

If I knew where, I might know who had been responsible for his disappearance. Because if they had made him talk, they sure as hell would be working the area in which he had found the gold chain and the coins with the strange pine-tar coating.

Jason Boone wasn't looking for the *Gaspar*. But

he was looking for the two fleet tenders which had gone down in the hurricane with it. He said they would be archaeologically significant. But because he had researched the fleet tenders, he also knew a great deal about the *Gaspar.*

"Six hundred million dollars' worth of gold and silver has brought a lot of very serious treasure hunters to the Marquesas," he had told me the morning before. "Add to that a few hundred million more from some of the other Spanish ships that went down there, and you can understand why people have been combing the area for treasure for more than three hundred years.

"The Spaniards were the first, Dusky. They didn't just write off the *Gaspar* as a complete loss. They sent a salvage team up from Cuba almost immediately. They had rustic diving bells, but even with those they couldn't retrieve much of it. Then the English came, the French, too—but no luck. After World War II, when scuba was finally perfected, the search continued. Divers found other wrecks, some treasure—even some of the brass cannon from the *Gaspar.* But no one could find the main lode. It's one of the great treasure-hunting mysteries of all time."

"Why a mystery?"

"Well, it's not, really. The reason no one has found it is pretty obvious. As you probably know, that area off the Marquesas is called the Quicksands for good reason. It's like an underwater desert: the currents are strong and the sand is continually shifting. By now the *Gaspar* and its treasure are buried in between twenty to thirty feet of sand. But someday, as the magnetometers improve and the dredging equipment gets better, someone will find it. And that person will immediately become one of the richest men on earth."

"But you're not interested?"

He had smiled wryly. "Hey, I'm only human. I'm the founder of an organization called Christ's Children of America, and with that much money we could . . . well, do some very good work. But I'm not a treasure hunter at heart. I'm an archaeologist."

I was jolted from my daydreaming by a hysterical whine from the magnetometer's beeper. I looked up, surprised—only about two miles off the low mangrove islands. I had my doubts about finding any underwater electronic devices—but this far from the Cuban shrimp boat?

I backed down both throttles immediately and scampered down the ladder to the deck. I threw over one bright-orange marker immediately, then, at dead slow, I circled back over the area, listening as the beeper got progressively louder. When it seemed as if my ears would burst, I tossed out another marker, switched the beeper off, and dropped anchor.

I was in about thirteen feet of water. Visibility didn't look good. It was milky turquoise in color, roiled by the tide. I thought about giving Stormin' Norman a call via the Key West marine operator, then realized just how silly that would be. VHF is the biggest party line on earth. Everybody listens.

I got my mask, fins, and snorkel out of the locker, then slipped over the side. There were a few sea fans on the bottom. A spider crab. A barracuda—about a three-footer—came in close to get a look at me.

Nothing else.

I surfaced, grabbed another bite of air, then swam underwater around the perimeter of the boat, along the bottom. And noticed something. Odd shapes beneath the sand. Too orderly. I climbed back up into the boat and got some equipment ready.

I carried a fresh bottle of air from the cabin— one of the big yellow Dacors—and slid enough lead onto my weight belt to hold me solidly on the bottom. And then I got the little folding shovel— ridiculously slow, but it was all I had.

Just as I was about to pull the back harness on, my VHF radio started squawking at me. "This is the motor vessel *Superior* calling the motor vessel *Sniper* . . . *Superior* calling the motor vessel *Sniper* . . ."

It was Wayne Peters calling me from Jason Boone's chartered boat.

"Hey, Dusky, I've been trying to get ahold of you all day."

"Been busy, Wayne. What's up?"

"Jason wants me to invite you to dinner tonight. Having a little beach party over on Fullmoon Cay." He laughed through a crackle of static. "And would you mind bringing a couple of extra beers for me? Kind of a dry trip with this group, if you know what I mean."

"No problem. Relief will be there around . . . sunset?"

"Perfect. Hope you're hungry. This is the *Superior*, clear."

I gave my call letters and signed off.

So, no beer on the Boone expedition. Taut ship. I smiled. I put a couple on ice for the blond wrestler from Iowa.

After checking my regulator, I pulled on tank, mask, fins, and weight belt and rolled off into the water. If you've ever tried to dig a hole underwater you know how tough it is. I sat on the sand bottom, legs spread wide, digging around one of the many oblong shapes. It took a while. A long while. But finally I hit something. Metal. Rust-colored, corroded. What kind of electronic device was this? It certainly wasn't new to the neighborhood. I cleared more of the sand away with my hands.

And then I stopped. Frozen. How could I have been so damn stupid?

Torpedo.

A whole line of them. And still live, apparently. I lifted the shovel carefully away. The bastards could go off at any time. Probably leftovers from some World War II practice session. They just took off and left them. Back in the forties, the Marquesas was the middle of nowhere. Who could they hurt?

Me, that's who. And any other fisherman, sport diver, or boater who just happened by at the wrong time.

Carefully, I pulled the quick-release buckle of my weight belt, inflated my lungs, and let the tide carry me slowly away to what I hoped would be safety. But it didn't.

The water deepened into the quick current of a tidal trough, like an underwater riverbed. More

strange shapes beneath the sand, and exposed
metal. Twisted hulk of a target vessel. Crater of a
recent explosion. Rusted globes of metal half covered by sand. Not ornaments, these. I recognized
them from my UDT training in Coronado. Old
magnetic explosives.

I had stumbled onto a whole damn minefield.

And I had too much steel strapped to me to let
myself get any closer. With smooth thrusts of fins,
I nosed back into the tide, surfacing slowly. I came
up by the first orange marker I had dropped and
swam back to *Sniper*.

I'd leave the markers and report what I had
found when I got back.

It was about time the Navy did something
about it.

Fullmoon Cay is a sweep of white beach backdropped by coconut palms and black mangroves
with a circular saltwater marsh in the middle. It's
a small island thick with prickly pear and bayonet
plants and, in the summer, bugs.

But now, in late October, it was the little coral-
water paradise you see in the picture postcards.
A good place to use your charge card and escape
to. A good place for lovers to walk hand in hand
on the beach and dance in moonlight.

Only there were no hotels on Fullmoon Cay. Or
airports. Or roads. No place to use the charge
card. It was small and deserted, not even shown
on most charts. And I could see why Jason Boone
had selected it as base camp. For his fresh-faced
kids from Iowa, it had to seem like paradise.

Their tents lined the beach in a bright multicolor

row of nylon; umbrella and geometric shapes in reds and greens and yellows against the white of the sand. There was a huge campfire throwing flames toward the steel-blue sunset sky, and a dozen or so young men and women waved at me as I nosed *Sniper* through the shallows off the beach and dropped anchor. They wore swimsuits. And smiles. They were playing touch football in the sand.

Wayne came up and shook my hand as I waded in. With his shirt off, you could see what kind of wrestler he must have been. His stomach was plated with muscle, his forearms looked like small thighs, and his shoulders were almost as wide as mine—and he was an inch or two shorter than I.

"They must raise kids right back in Davenport," I said.

He winked at me—that big, funny wink. "It's all that corn they feed us. Hey, Jason's up by the fire. Wait till you see what we're having for supper."

I followed him past the others. They'd gone back to their laughing-splashing game. About half of them were girls. It was hard not to notice. Four blonds and two redheads, all dressed in flower-colored nylon swimsuits. They looked like alternate Miss Americas on vacation. I watched one of the redheads do a quick down-and-out pattern, her breasts bouncing hypnotically. The pass was wide and low. She made an amazing diving catch, jumped up, and spiked the ball, grinning triumphantly. The others applauded, pounding her on the back.

Wayne noticed me watching. "Nice scenery, huh?"

"I think I'm becoming a football fan."

"And there are five more just as pretty back in Key West. Not enough room."

"Wayne, I'm not one of those snobs about physical appearance, but I just can't help noticing that there's not an unattractive person here—male or female. Where'd Jason come up with this group?"

He shrugged. "Lot of the Born Agains seem to come from upper-class families. Things too easy for 'em, I guess. They get restless and turn to God. Have you ever noticed that there aren't very many ugly rich kids?"

"Never thought about it, but I guess you're right."

He grinned. "Not that I'm complaining! Jason's helped them all a lot, and we all think the world of him. Every one of those kids out there is being trained to go into administrative work for the C.C.A. It's good work, too."

"And what about you?"

"So far I'm just a student of history. I love it. I haven't felt the call to join the fellowship yet, but . . ." He winked again. "If heaven is anything like this place, I just might."

Jason was tending an impressive pile of lobster tails by the fire. He seemed happy to see me. He wore cutoff jeans and a copper-colored crew-neck T-shirt that went well with his beard and hair. Wayne started to leave, and I remembered something. "Hey, Wayne! That book you wanted me to bring is in the cabin of my boat. Help yourself."

He grinned. "Thanks, Dusky. And don't forget, you promised to tell me about the SEALs later."

We watched him trot out toward the water, muscles in sharp relief with every stride.

"There goes one of the most impressive young people I've ever met, Dusky. Terrific personality, a truly brilliant student, and one of the finest wrestlers ever to come out of Iowa—and that's saying something." He reached down with a long fork and turned one row of lobster cooking on a grate over the coals.

"You seem somehow disappointed, the way you said that."

His bright-blue eyes caught mine, and he nodded. "Is it that obvious? Yeah, I guess it is. I keep forgetting—we have too much in common to fool each other."

"So what's the problem with Wayne?"

"Well, there are a couple of little things. He has a terrible temper, for one thing. He doesn't seem to enjoy fighting, but if someone gets him mad—look out."

"Sounds like you might be describing a younger version of Jason Boone."

He poked at the lobster with a reflective smile. "I'm afraid you're right. Maybe that's why I like him so much—he reminds me of the way I was. But I feel I could do so much with him, Dusky, if he would just . . ."

"See the light?"

He shook his head. "This is just between you and me, but if Wayne would just open his heart and let the Lord come into it, the religious organization I founded—the C.C.A.—would be his one day. And it's already grown tremendously. We have a pretty widely televised fund-raising ministry and an international radio ministry. And with Wayne at the controls, I would know that it would keep getting bigger and better."

"I would have thought you'd be saving that roll for your own children, Jase."

The sudden stoicism which took his face carried more visual impact than the pain it certainly covered. "It was a nasty, useless war we fought, Dusky. I came back with Purple Hearts and absolutely no chance of having kids."

"I'm sorry, Jase."

"You don't have to be sorry, Dusky. You were there." The sudden wry smile surprised me, snubbing a very uncomfortable moment. "Let us two old soldiers call those youngsters to supper, then sit around and tell stories. Not the bloody kind. Just stories." He slapped me on the back. "But watch out you don't get trampled in the rush."

I was charmed by this guy: big and brutal-looking, but intelligent, and he had style. The religious ones usually make me uncomfortable. I keep worrying they're going to try to "save" me. And, frankly, I just don't want to be saved. It's my childish independent streak, I guess. I don't want to belong to any group—even if it is God's. But I don't try to fool myself. If the Bible is right—and a lot of very smart people like Jason Boone believe it is—they're not just going to give me a forgiving smile and a kindly reprieve when I reach the Pearly Gates. They're going to send my ass to Hell. I've sent too many human beings there myself to get off scot-free. But Jason didn't make me feel uncomfortable. I had a feeling that if he did try to save me, it wouldn't be an embarrassing session of one-sided preaching. It would at least be intelligent conversation.

It was a fine evening—and Jason was right about his group. When they came to eat it was all business. There was plenty of lobster, whole baked grouper, raw oysters from the bar in the lagoon, and plenty of melted butter and hot sauce. No beer, but what the hell. It was dark by the time we were all done, and we sat in the busy night sounds of the sea and the island and the crackle of the fire. It was time for talk; relaxed conversation, with everyone included. I told them about fishing, and what it was like to be a guide. They laughed at the right places. The faces of the dozen or so kids hung suspended above the fire, their blue or green eyes soft with contentment. I noticed that they had paired off. Some of the guys had their arms around their girls. At least Jason allowed that—I had noticed a look of reproach when Wayne accepted the little tin of Copenhagen I had offered. He seemed to be a stern but kindly master. When he ordered the pots and dishes cleaned up, they all moved with the speed and efficiency of Marines readying for a firefight.

Or Green Berets.

There was a military orderliness about them all; an orderliness tempered, it seemed, by the love of some common cause.

If this was religion, it didn't seem bad.

Wayne was the only guy not sitting with a girl. I noticed the redhead who had made the spectacular catch earlier eyeing him. He didn't seem to pay much attention. I moved around to the other side of the fire and sat by him. By that time, Jason had brought out a guitar and handed it to a tall blond girl with extremely long hair and a lithe body. She played something soft—some Christian folksong I had never heard before. It had an easy refrain, and some of the others around the fire joined in:

> *Come with Him.*
> *He has chosen us*
> *To win our peace*
> *The chosen must. . . .*

It was a haunting melody, pretty in the softness of the night.

"Looks like you have an admirer over there, Wayne."

He looked up from the fire. "Oh, yeah." He blushed a little. "That's Jennifer. Nice kid."

"That's all. Nice?"

He eyed me askance. "Hey, MacMorgan, don't you turn matchmaker on me now. One around here is enough."

"I have competition?"

"Jason can't believe I've been around her two weeks and haven't stolen her off to my tent yet."

"That doesn't sound like Jason."

"That's the good thing about him, really. He's real strict in some ways, and not so strict in others—if you know what I mean."

I looked across the fire at the redhead, Jennifer. She was one handsome article indeed. "I can't believe you even need a push."

"I guess that's one of my biggest character flaws. Someone pushes, I immediately push back. She's a great person, don't get me wrong. National AAU swimming champion, graduated cum laude and all that." He gave me another of those winks. " 'Course, if I get any hornier, I might just take Jason's advice. But if I do it'll be because I want to."

"I think one of you has already made the decision."

"I know, she stares at me all the time. Hey, let's go for a walk before I finally make any momentous decisions."

We walked down along the water. I waded out, got a couple of beers, and we sat in the moonlight talking. Good man, Wayne Peters. He told me about growing up in a little town called North Scott, Iowa. Farm boy. Mother died when he was fourteen. His great recreations when the work was done were books and sports. Wayne had that unaffected honesty you find in very few people. I broke a rule. He asked me about the SEALs and Vietnam. And I told him. Occasionally I meet some rare person who can handle the truth without oohing and aahing. Sometimes I meet someone who deserves to know.

He said nothing when I had finished.

"I'm not the only one on this island who knows about Nam, Wayne."

"Jason."

"Did he ever talk to you about it?"

"Yeah. I guess I was the only one in the whole group who he told. I felt like I feel now—sort of honored."

"He thinks very highly of you."

"I know. And it bothers me. I'm going to disappoint him, Dusky. I just can't join the flock. You know? I just can't. I'm not a . . . believer. I don't mind leading the prayers, and handling all the responsibility he gives me. But I just can't make myself believe. And because of that, I'm still an outsider. Twice a week they have their C.C.A. prayer meetings. I could attend if I asked to, but I haven't asked. That used to leave me with just Abbey to talk to. Now it leaves me by myself— which I like a lot better."

"Other than that, you get along okay, don't you?"

"Sure. Jason has sort of made me his right-hand man. I admire the guy, I really do. He's had some awful things happen to him, but he's always landed on his feet. In a way, I worry about him. Because he's religious, people may think they can shove him around. I don't know if you realize it, Dusky, but there are some real jerks hunting for treasure around here. There used to be this funny-looking old guy in a small boat who'd follow us around. I'd work for days getting an underwater grid set up on a wreck we'd found, and this old guy would dive on it later and screw it up."

"I knew that old guy, Wayne. He disappeared out here. I think he was murdered."

"What? Look, I'm sorry, Dusky. I didn't know. He just left one day and never came back."

"It's okay. Who are some of the other jerks?"

"Well, the biggest one is a guy who's hunting an area a few miles west and south of here. He's a great big guy, and nasty as hell. Threatened to shoot Jason and me one day."

"And what did you do?"

"Lost my temper, naturally—another big character flaw of mine. Told him I'd come back and stick that gun in his ear."

I laughed and told him why I would have a new scar thanks to Buster Ronstadz.

"Geez, I wish I had been there with you."

"Me too, Wayne. Me too."

"I'm telling you, Dusky, there are some strange things going on around here at night. I don't trust any of those people."

"How so?"

"Well, I don't sleep too well. Never have. So when I can't sleep I usually jump in one of the skiffs and go offshore. I stick out a bait and just drift and think and look at the stars. There's a salvage barge out there operated by a bunch of Cuban-Americans. And they're always moving around at night. I watch their lights. One night they sent over a boat to one of the magnetometer pegs we had worked earlier that day. They sent down divers. Underwater lights and everything. I told Jason, and he said not to worry about it. That Buster guy is always sending spies over to our sites to nose around. Jason spent a couple of nights out there, keeping a watch, but nothing ever came of it. To tell you the truth, I've taken my skiff out to their boats at night just to listen— to sort of get even, you know. I just run way up-tide and drift back down on them. They never even know I'm there."

"Sounds dangerous. Or foolish."

"Stupid is what it was. There was just something in me that made me do it. I wanted to hear what they'd found out about us. But I never did hear anything worth a damn."

"I think you would have made a good SEAL, Wayne."

"You know something, Dusky? That means a lot to me."

I awoke in darkness. Someone had come aboard, onto *Sniper*. I felt her list ever so slightly. I threw back my covers and reached under the pillow to find the pleasant chill of my Randall attack-survival knife. Outside, through the glass port, the fire still smoldered on the beach. The tents were ghostly chunks of darkness in the pale moonlight. *Sniper* listed again, then rolled on the gentle groundswell.

I stood behind the door and waited.

Someone walked across the aft deck, coming closer. When the silhouette was full frame in the little window, I jerked the door open, grabbed a wrist, then swung the uninvited visitor down to the floor, my knife at his neck.

"Hey! Hold it!"

The voice wasn't a he. It was a she. I flipped on a light.

It was the redhead, Jennifer.

"Some welcome! I just came to ask . . ." She stopped and I saw an interesting smile cross her face. And then I realized—I was naked. I turned my back and pulled on shorts.

"What in the hell do you think you're doing, woman? That's a good way to get killed."

She had her hand on her mouth, trying not to laugh. "Geez, you're something!"

"Just tell me what you're doing out here so I can get back to sleep."

It sobered her. "It's Wayne, Dusky. He's not in his tent. I thought he might be out here."

"Well, he's not. He probably couldn't sleep and went out fishing or something." She was making me nervous. She wore the same flower-colored nylon swimsuit. She had gotten wet coming out to the boat. It was see-through in the cabin light: round globes of breasts and the fibrous outline of pubic hair.

"Can I ask you something, Dusky?"

"What!"

"Wayne trusts you. I saw the way you two were talking tonight. Does he . . . dislike me for some reason?"

"He likes you fine. Now go to bed."

"Do you . . . do you like me, Dusky?"

"You're aces with me, Jennifer. Now go to bed and shut the door behind you."

I switched off the light. I heard the door shut. But she hadn't gone. She was still for a moment, then slid into bed with me. She was naked. I started to speak, and she covered my lips with hers. She tasted of salt and smelled of tanning lotion.

"I'm going to give you until the count of three to get out of here."

Her small hand found me beneath the covers, and she held me gently. I pulled the hand away.

"One!"

"What is it with you two! Am I that unattractive!"

"Two!"

"You don't understand the way it is!" Her anger quickly turned to tears. She lay there crying silently. I stroked her soft hair.

"Jennifer, you know you're not unattractive. And believe me, I do understand how it is. But not me, not now. I promise I won't tell another soul, not even Wayne, if you go now."

She touched my lips softly with hers and was gone.

14

Someone was screaming. Terrified scream. It slid into my sleep and my dream embraced it. Back in the jungle. Back in the heat and the darkness and the stench of death. Too many piles; too many stacks of ruined arms and faces and legs and I could never, ever put them all back together again . . .

I sat bolt upright, eyes blinking in the fresh light of morning.

The scream was no dream. Someone outside, on the beach. A woman's scream.

I ran from the cabin. The blond kids scurried from their tents, running.

Over here! Someone . . . please!

I jumped over the side and half ran, half swam to shore. High tide.

It was Jennifer. The group gathered around her, on the sand. She stood in water up to her calfs, her hand to her mouth. They were looking at something washed ashore by the weak surf. It was a body, facedown. Big form fluttering in the wash and draw of sea, blond hair fluttering like seaweed.

Damn! Not Wayne . . .

I busted through the little group of horrified kids. Jennifer leaned against me as if about to faint. "Dusky, it's not . . ." I studied the body closely from where we stood. Too much fat on the sides. Too much bloated belly.

"No," I said. "No, it's not Wayne."

"Oh, thank you, Jesus . . ."

I told the kids to move back. With my foot, I turned the body over. A small blue crab skittered sideways across the battered face. I recognized what was left of it. Buster Ronstadz. The big bad wife-beating bully. Buster had run into someone he couldn't push around. The bone structure of his face was a collapsed jumble of bruises and purple flesh. The nose was sideways. One eye was gone. The crab was upset. It hadn't gotten a chance to finish its work. It plopped huffily into the surf and swam away. Buster's mouth was open as if frozen in a scream. The tongue was swollen and swung animal-like with the motion of the waves.

"You people get back to your duties—now!"

It was Jason. There was still toothpaste on his beard. He came trotting down toward us. "No questions. Move!" There were no questions. They stiffened like soldiers and left immediately. They were oddly silent in the turquoise dawn of Fullmoon Cay.

"God help us," said Jason. "God help us all . . ."

It was one rude awakening; one ugly way to start the day.

"Is that . . ."

"Yeah, it's Ronstadz."

I didn't like the way my mind was working. I didn't like what I was thinking.

"Where's Wayne?"

Jason thought for a moment. "I haven't seen him this morning. Wasn't he on the beach with the others?"

"No. I want to talk to him."

Some nasty facts were beginning to click in my head. Wayne didn't like my troublesome old friend, Gifford Remus. And he had been very upset when he heard about my little run-in with Buster.

"My God, Dusky, you don't think . . ."

"I don't know, Jason. You mentioned Wayne's temper. How bad was it?"

"Well, he would go sort of wild—but no worse than the rest of us."

"The last time you went 'sort of wild,' Jason, you broke a man's neck."

He sagged, horror-struck. "I can't believe it . . . I can't believe what's happening. Not Wayne . . . he was so, so perfect . . ."

I could picture the invitation in the Christ's Children of America literature: "Join us in the tropical Florida Keys for an enjoyable and enlightening archaeological experience with fellow young Christians. . . ."

But Wayne Peters had been an outsider. He couldn't make himself believe. And suddenly things were going very, very sour indeed.

Wait a minute, MacMorgan.

I made myself stop. Some jury I was. I had

thrown together some circumstantial evidence and already found the kid guilty. Some friend I turned out to be. I liked Wayne Peters. He was a kindred spirit, one of the very few I had ever met. So at least give him a chance.

"Jason, I'm probably wrong. I hope I'm wrong. But I think we'd better find Wayne and have a talk with him."

But Wayne wasn't on the island. Nor aboard the *Sniper* or Jason's chartered steel-hulled salvage boat. I found Jennifer and asked her. She was in her tent reading the Bible. She seemed to have already recovered.

"Dusky, I waited up for him. Almost all night. But he never came back."

"You're sure?"

She gave me an odd smile. "I think you know better than anyone how, ah, anxious I was to find him. I would have known."

I stood with the flap of her tent pushed back. "That was not a very pretty sight down there. Are you feeling better?"

She held up the book she was reading. "I have to learn not to question Him. It was His work."

If it was His work, He had done one thorough job of it.

I found Jason again. He was talking to a half-dozen or so of his group beneath the screened meeting tent. I felt that I was interrupting. He came outside when I motioned.

"Jason, I'm going to take care of the body, then make a tour around the area in my boat and look for Wayne."

He nodded soberly, still in shock. I put my

hands on his big shoulders and shook him gently. "Look, we'll get this thing worked out. These kids look to you for strength. Don't let them down, okay?"

"You're right, Dusky, you're right. But the thought of Wayne doing *that* . . ."

"Jason, all you have to do is get hold of the Coast Guard on VHF. Just tell them what we've found and tell them to send someone out. I'll handle everything else."

He put one huge hand on mine. "I appreciate it, Dusky. I really do." He looked into my eyes. "You're a good man, MacMorgan. One of these days I hope we'll work together. I hope you'll come around to the Lord . . ."

"Save it for later, Jason. We'll talk about it."

I pulled the corpse of Buster Ronstadz by the feet up above the high-tide line. I hadn't liked him. I doubted if his wife even did. But some young mother had suckled him and played with him and dreamed good dreams for his future. And no one deserved the sort of beating he had taken. The weight of death fills you with despair. It leaches a little of the breath from your lungs and returns it as a cold brain wind that whispers of your own mortality. But I had to put my thoughts of the cosmos aside when I held my nose and bent down to go through dead Buster's pockets. Soggy cigarettes. A plastic lighter. And then something else: one strange crested silver coin caked with pine tar. It was like those I had found in Gifford Remus's camp. And just what in the hell did it mean? Stain of the Marquesas; it had suddenly become one bloody place to be. But I didn't have time to worry about it.

Buster Ronstadz's boat was an oil- and rust-stained scow called *Li'l Hustler*. It was an old sportfisherman whose time had come and gone. Using the radar, I vectored in on it. It floated grimy white on the blue-green shimmer of open sea. They flew a diver-down flag, and I circled it slowly from a distant perimeter. When I caught the eye of a man on the flybridge, I pointed at the water with a quizzical expression. He tried to wave me away, but I was insistent. Finally, he gave me the okay sign and waved me in.

"You better have a good reason for being here, mister." It was a chubby Italian guy with a nose that had suffered from too many long nights with the bottle. His T-shirt was gray with sweat.

"Your buddy Ronstadz is dead." I watched his face closely for change of expression.

"You trying to be funny?"

"Not hardly."

He shook his head and exhaled slowly. "And that bastard owes me a bunch of money, too."

Three more men came up onto the deck. They were a nasty-looking bunch. One of them carried a pistol behind his back, trying to hide it. I said, "I hate to bother you in your time of grief, but you wouldn't have any idea who did it, would you? He was beaten to death."

"You a cop, or what?"

"Just a concerned citizen."

"Then don't get cute with me, buddy. That bas-

tard ain't worth cryin' over. The last time we saw
him, he was gettin' in the skiff to go pay a visit
on the spic treasure hunters over there."

"Why?"

He sneered at me. "In the treasure-huntin' business, mister, you got to keep an eye on the
competition."

"We've already contacted the Coast Guard. If
you want to claim the body, it's—"

"We ain't claimin' nothing, buddy. What we're
gonna do is haul anchor and head back into Key
West and sell this piece of shit for whatever we
can get for it." He spit in the water at me. "Now
why don't you mosey on along and mind your
own business, huh?"

The guy with the pistol stepped forward, bran-
dishing it awkwardly. Pimply-faced kid with a big
revolver; some kind of cheap .357.

"Couple of more things before the shooting
starts."

He chuckled at my brazenness. "Yeah."

"Did you see a blond kid in a skiff go by here?"

"No. Anything else, buddy?"

"Yeah. Tell pizza-face there to load his weapon
next time he wants to act tough."

I pegged full throttles and left the *Li'l Hustler*
rolling in *Sniper*'s sudden wake. Childish show-
down. But I was in no mood for the down-and-
out media tough guys. They swagger around with
.357s because that's what that magnum-force guy
always uses, and, man oh man, did you see him
blow all those guys away? We're all becoming
ragtag collages of too many bad film dramas. Television sucks out our own personalities and re-

places them with bits and pieces from prime time. Depending on the situation, we all fall into the hypnotic roles pounded into our heads five nights a week. I fear for the kids. They spend their creative years glued to the TV's comforting glow, their eyes wide, absorbing it all. And when reality confronts them, their subconscious kicks in like a generator, and they become Archie or John Boy or Richie and the Fonz, or Barney Miller or sweet sweet Cissy with her pendulum tits. Or Dirty Harry.

No, I wasn't in the mood. Maybe it was guilt. If Wayne had done what I hoped he hadn't, maybe it was because I had nudged him into the roll of the big bad SEAL with my war stories. Damn the stories. Damn the roles. I took the tin of Copenhagen from my shirt and took a comforting pinch. And damn the person who tried to get in my way.

The Cuban shrimp boat was a green bleep on the radar screen as I headed offshore, toward Marquesas Rock. They had anchored up again. Quiet time. I circled them once and gave a couple of blasts on the horn. Finally a small Cuban man in a loose blue blouse stepped out, rubbing the sleep from his eyes. He smiled. Waved.

"Hola, amigo!"

I tried my bad Spanish. Had he seen a guy with hair *muy blanco* go by in a skiff?

He shrugged and shook his head. No.

"Hola, amigo!"

Same smile. Same shake of the head. Another man came onto the deck. Tall, no-nonsense type. He wasn't smiling. And he sure as hell wasn't

Cuban. He looked Arabic. He said something to
the little man in rapid Spanish. I heard the words
Vamos ahora! Time to leave. I had the magnetometer tethered behind on a short line. I switched on
the little radio beeper and made another circle
around the shrimp boat, smiling my best mixed-
up smile. The name of the boat was *Jose Martí.*
The beeper didn't make a sound.

Where in the hell could Wayne be? It didn't
make any sense. Maybe he had killed Ronstadz in
a fight, gotten scared, and headed back to Key
West to make a run for it. I hoped that wasn't
it. He was too smart a kid to ruin his life with
one mistake.

I had one last stop to make. The Cuban-
American salvage barge, *Libertad.* It was a large
low-freeboard hulk hard at work. They had twin
underwater blowers on, running off the propel-
lers, and the green water was turgid with silt
when I arrived. They had divers down, so I approached well off their bow and sounded my horn
to let them know I was coming.

And they didn't exactly welcome me with
open arms.

Two guys came running out, waving me away,
as I tried to nose in close enough to be heard.
They both wore sidearms. One guy pulled out
what looked like a .45 Enforcer and surprised me
by popping a few rounds into the water. The slugs
didn't miss the hull of *Sniper* by much.

As I said, I was in no mood. I had had my
fill of being put off and pushed around by the
hardnoses, the self-appointed tough guys. He

squeezed off one more round when I refused to back off, and that was that. I reached over and grabbed the brutal AK-47 assault automatic I had mounted in spring clips above the wheel, swung *Sniper* around with a thrust of starboard throttle, and outlined the bow of the barge with a thunderous burst of my own—and noticed, at the same time, that there was a seventeen-foot mako lashed to their port side. I recognized the skiff.

It was one of two Jason Boone's group had anchored off Fullmoon Cay.

When the roar of the assault rifle silenced, the two guys on the bow put their sidearms away, looking a little meek. It's the way I wanted them to look. Suddenly someone shut down the underwater blowers. And in the new quiet, a tall, well-dressed Cuban came striding up. He didn't look happy.

"I want your name, and the name of your vessel! This incident will be reported to the Coast Guard!"

"Your men opened up on me first."

"They thought they had seen a shark. They were mistaken."

"And I thought I saw the same shark."

He eyed me in reassessment. I could almost see the wheels turning. He was tall for a Cuban. Thin, but muscled beneath the expensive sports shirt. He wore a gold diver's watch, and thin gold chains around his neck. Finally he said: "You're not welcome here, gringo. We have a permit for this area. You're trespassing. And I insist that you either give me your name, or leave immediately."

He had the stance of the insulted businessman. I had interrupted their work and upset his people. Shame on me. He was going to tell.

"Okay, partner. Sure. My name's MacMorgan. Dusky MacMorgan. And your name's Emanuel Ortiz—no, don't ask me how I know." I leveled the assault rifle at his nose. "Now it's your turn to talk. Emanuel is going to tell Dusky why he has that little mako tied up when it belongs to someone else. And Emanuel is going to talk real fast or he's going to spend eternity saying grace through his asshole."

He didn't scare easy, but it shook him. As I talked, I saw the other men arming themselves, moving. Jason was right. It was a well-organized group. Ortiz's people moved as if they knew what they were doing. And they had the weapons. There's a blunt, stark efficiency to the look of Russian armaments. And, aside from a few sidearms, they were all Russian.

Ortiz knew his people were readying themselves. He thought the tide had turned. He almost smiled. "Perhaps, Mr. MacMorgan, you would like to tell me what business it is of yours."

"A friend of mine was in that boat. Now my friend has disappeared. And by the way, Ortiz— if one of your men so much as makes a loud noise, or a move I don't understand, your head's coming right off."

He cleared his throat nervously. "They're better trained than that, Mr. MacMorgan. But about your friend—I'm afraid we don't know a thing. We found the boat adrift early this morning. We thought it belonged to the man who was killed last night. We were holding it for the Coast Guard."

"And how do you know about that?"

He pointed at my radio antenna. "You really should keep your VHF switched on, Mr. MacMorgan. A vessel named *Superior* contacted the authorities this morning. You learn all sorts of things on the VHF, Mr. MacMorgan." He finished with an odd smile.

Another standoff.

Damn.

"I don't suppose you would let me come aboard—just in the event you somehow overlooked my friend?"

"I wish I could, but we really don't have the time. Another day, perhaps."

Mock answer to a mock question. But if Wayne didn't show up, I'd have my day. And Emanuel Ortiz could bet on it.

"I'll send someone back to pick up the mako," I said.

"You do that, Mr. MacMorgan. But tell whoever comes to watch out for the sharks. They're everywhere out here."

15

It was nearing dusk when I saw Wayne Peters high-tailing it across the reef in the little mako toward my anchorage off the Marquesas. I'll always remember because the explosion was the same blood-red hue of the sunset sky.

Someone seemed to be chasing him. He kept looking back at his own wake and pointing. He held his head at an odd angle as if he was hurt. There was a dark line of something dripping down his face, and in the wind and the sunlight, his hair was a crimson mane.

I was surprised to see him. And happy, too. I felt good that he was turning to me for help.

But I was even more surprised at what happened when he got across the reef.

After my little interlude with the Cuban-Americans, I had run back to Fullmoon Cay. Jason seemed to have recovered, but he was still worried about Wayne. They had called off work for the day. Everyone was too upset. I told him about my meetings, and he flared when I told him that his little mako was being held by the *Libertad.* He wanted to go after it right away, but he agreed, finally, that he should just wait for the Coast Guard boat that was being sent to pick up the body of Buster Ronstadz. Little did we know that the Coast Guard would have two bodies to pick up.

I showed him the Spanish coin I had taken from Ronstadz's body. He turned it this way and that, studying it. He even went into his tent and got a magnifying glass.

"Very interesting," he had said. "It's a Spanish real. Struck in Mexico probably in the 1620s, I'd say. But the unusual thing is that it is in absolutely perfect condition." He was enjoying himself. You could tell he loved his work. It took his mind off everything else, and for a few moments he was without worry, telling me about that coin.

"You see, Dusky, gold doesn't tarnish underwater. But silver does. In salt water, silver creates an electrolytic current which forms silver sulfide. There's usually a black patina covering anything silver."

"So that means it wasn't found underwater?"

"Not necessarily. You see these little bits of gummy substance? Well, it wasn't too unusual for the Spaniards to sneak back contraband along with their regular treasure manifest. And to get contraband coins past the queen's customs people, they'd sometimes hide them in barrels of pitch."

"So it is pine tar?"

"Probably. You look disappointed."

I told him about finding similar coins at Gifford Remus's camp.

"And you thought finding this coin on Ronstadz cleared up the mystery of the old man's disappearance." He thought for a moment. "Maybe Ronstadz did kill him. Or maybe the old man just drowned and Ronstadz stole them from his camp. But it's just as likely that Ronstadz found it himself. As I said—it wasn't all that unusual. Interesting, but not unique."

We had had a nice talk then. Jason had deep feelings, deep convictions, about almost everything. He seemed sincerely concerned about America, the economy, the bulging welfare rolls, and the race riots. We talked about the things all people talk about, and it was a pleasant, comfortable time. I could see why he had been so successful. He's one of the rare ones with a charismatic personality and the physical presence to go along with it. He was Senate material. Or even presidential.

So I had headed back to my own anchorage. I had work to do. I wanted to keep a real tight eye on the Cuban-Americans, and maybe even pay them a late-night visit. It would be a good evening for it. The radio was talking storm warnings in the Florida Straits, and the wind had swung around out of the north, gusting, chilled.

It was going to storm, all right. I went to the little beach on the Marquesas to check around Gifford's camp one more time and watch the storm take the island. There was nothing to find. Dead campfire.

And that's when I saw Wayne coming across the reef. I stood up and waved both arms back and forth. He spotted me. He seemed relieved. He had found sanctuary. I was the big tough SEAL, the kindred spirit, the older friend who was going to help save him from . . . something. Even holding his head at the odd angle, hair bloodied in the storm wind, he smiled.

And that's when his world exploded.

It was a single crimson blast. The storm blew the noise away from me, and it sounded oddly impotent. A bright-red *whewfff* backdropped by the leaden red of the squall sunset. I felt as if I was dreaming. One hell of a bad dream. The skiff didn't lift from the water; it splintered in a ball of flame, going in every direction. In the slow-motion horror of the moment, that somehow bothered me. My mind had hooked on one instant explanation— he had hit one of the free-floating mines. But the boat wasn't lifted from the water.

Wayne was.

He went tumbling over the water like some gruesome rag doll. The remains of the boat melted in flames behind him, casting strange colors across the leaden sea. It seemed as if I was in the little Whaler headed for him almost before he hit.

He was an amazing young man. He was still alive, not about to give up without a fight. But he was ruined. I held him in my arms as he struggled against it.

"Who, Wayne? Who?"

"Cu . . . Cubans . . ."

His blue eyes were crossed and his hair smoldered. He died with a half smile, trying to wink at me. . . .

I told Jason first, of course. I had wrapped the body in the best canvas I had aboard and headed for Fullmoon Cay in a daze. I tried to get ahold of Norm Fizer through the marine operator on the way. No answer and try back please, sir.

Right. Absolutely.

But I was going to shake some people up first.

Jason's eyes changed when I told him. He looked like a troubled kid, sleepwalking.

"It wasn't an accident? I just can't believe that someone . . . are you sure?"

"Jason, I know explosives. It was some kind of bomb. Maybe radio-activated. Maybe just a stick of dynamite on the ignition with a bad wiring job so it went off later than planned. But I checked the wreckage. The explosion was in the boat, not under it."

We stood on the beach in gray light. He had his hands in his pockets and his red beard swung flaglike in the storm wind. It was starting to sprinkle, and you could see the green veil of rain sweeping toward us on the sea.

"I have to tell the group. I guess I have no choice. My God, Dusky, what's happening?" He started to walk up the beach to the camp, then stopped. He turned to me. "You're not thinking about going after them, are you, Dusky?"

"Yes, Jason, I am."

"There's been too much violence already. I can't let you. It's a matter for the police, Dusky. The Coast Guard will be here soon . . . storm held them up . . . too much violence." He was muttering.

"Jason, Jason! Listen to me. There's something I haven't told you. I'm not really a treasure hunter, Jason. In a way, I am the police. I was sent out here, Jason. And I'm going."

He looked at me a moment, then turned and walked up the beach.

They had a service for Wayne, in the meeting tent. I could see the glow of their Coleman lanterns through the slashing rain and sudden brightness of lightning.

Jason preached. I could hear his voice sometimes carried to me on the wind. I sat soaking on the beach, watching *Sniper* and the sleek *Superior* swing nervously on their anchor lines. It was a black scudding storm sky, the speed of the clouds gauged by a reluctant moon.

I sat there thinking, wanting to be alone. I heard the group chanting a prayer, saying goodbye in their own way. And I could hear Jason above them all in the occasional silences of storm and wind. He preached as if angry.

He had every right to be angry.

Someone came up behind me and sat down on the wet sand. It was Jennifer. She wore a bright-yellow rain slicker. She reached out, and I let her take my hand.

"He had to go, you know."

"What?"

"Jesus called him. He had to go."

She was like a pathetic little girl. I said nothing. Frankly, I get a little tired hearing about God's mysterious ways. If there is a God, He's got one hell of a weird sense of humor.

"He was a good man, Jennifer."

"Yes. I wanted to have his babies."

I let that one pass and said, "I suppose you all will be heading back tomorrow, huh?"

"I don't know, Dusky, I just don't know." And

then: "Jason would like you to come up to the tent. It would make him feel better. He likes you, Dusky. He likes you a lot."

Sure, sure. Good old Dusky MacMorgan. Everybody likes Dusky.

They even smile when they die in his arms.

So I went up to the tent. The kids were lighting candles. They stuck one in my hand. Jennifer sat down beside me on the canvas floor. Jason stood before us at a little altar. Some of the kids, guys and girls, sobbed quietly.

Jason held up two candles, staring at them.

"One bright white light has left us," he said. He leaned and blew out one of the flames. "Yet there is still light. In his own way, Wayne Peters was an example to us all. In his own way, Wayne was an inspiration to us all."

Jason put his candle on the altar and motioned with his eyes toward one of the kids. The lithe blond went out into the storm and returned with her guitar. She played the same haunting melody as before, and everyone sang along. I started to stand and leave, but Jennifer took my hand again. When I sat back down, she leaned against me, crying.

They sang other songs. There was the sweet sad kinship among them of the living mourning their recent dead. They sat in a tight circle, I among them. Two violent deaths in one day. I looked at the pretty young faces in the candlelight and thought: This is one hell of a way for them to learn of the brutality. The poor, poor bastards.

The blond was just starting the chords of a final hymn when Jason suddenly jumped to his feet.

"Listen!"

The way he said it made my hair rise. There was only the roar of the storm and the wind in the trees—but then I heard it, too.

The thin sound of an engine. Someone was in a boat near the island.

Quickly I went running outside, right behind Jason. It was raining harder now. In the explosion of lightning, you could see the green rage of sea and white waves. And you could see a boat, too. A white skiff battling its way away from the rolling anchorage of *Sniper* and the *Superior*.

"They were messing with our boats!" Jason took off running toward the water. I swam out with him.

They were on our boats, all right. They had sledged my radio, and my rifle was gone.

And that's not the only thing they had taken.

Wayne's body was gone.

Jason stood behind me, hands on his hips, breathing deeply. Beneath the salon light, there was a wild look in his eyes. This wasn't the preacher, the humanitarian. He was someone from far, far away and long ago. He was back in the jungle again.

"You say you're going out there tonight, Dusky?"

"I'm going to make a point of it."

"That Cuban-American boat—they were pretty well armed."

"Sounds like a job for a SEAL."

"Yeah," said Jason. "A SEAL and one old Green Beret."

16

It was all a mistake.

A very fatal mistake.

I should have realized. I should have known. But while your body ages and turns slack and slow, your mind refuses to concede. We could overcome the guards and demand information. We could use strong-arm tactics because Jason was a Green Beret and, dammit, I was an invincible SEAL.

Was.

In truth, we were Don Quixote and Sancho. Old fools on mounts of our own imagination. But the Cubans were too well armed, too well trained. They were ready and waiting. And I was the biggest fool of all.

Oh, we planned our mission. We went over every detail like good soldiers. Jason had gone back to his tent and changed into khaki pants and black sweater. He carried his diving gear and an inflatable raft over one huge shoulder when he boarded *Sniper.* I handed him the olive-drab tube of face black, and we talked softly in the rage of storm as I fired up the big twin engines.

"I hate to admit it, Dusky, but I'm looking forward to this. I . . . I missed it so. . . ."

"I know what you mean, Jason. I know exactly what you mean."

We ran in stealth. No lights. The twelve-inch sweep of radar screen threw a soft green light across Jason's dark face. I told him how the *Libertad* was situated. I explained all I had been authorized to about my mission. He didn't seem as surprised as I had expected.

"Remember, Dusky, I spent some long years in that kind of service. I know how those things work. When you told me you were 'kind of a policeman' I started putting two and two together."

So we made our plans, went over the options. Jason offered suggestions. He was good. He knew the business. He insisted we not kill anyone unless it was absolutely necessary. I agreed—reluctantly. They might be Castro agents, but they were still American citizens. And their unexplained deaths could lead to some very nasty publicity.

I ran *Sniper* well downstorm of where the *Libertad* would be. Jason was a good mate. He dropped the anchor while I handled the throttle. In a flare of lightning, I could see him clearly on the bow, soaking but ready. It had been a long time since I had worked with someone else of commando quality. Too long. He looked back in at me and gave me a thumbs-up. He felt it, too. It was a good feeling. When the line was snubbed off and I was sure we had a solid hookup, we went over our equipment.

D. Harold Westervelt, as always, had done a thorough job. Nonlethal weapons, mostly. Jason was happy about that. He selected the Webber 4-B dart pistol with its twenty-six lignum vitae darts loaded with a knockout drug. I told him that the drug could sometimes work too slow for hundred-percent efficency. I knew all too well about that. But he didn't seem to mind. Hidden aboard *Sniper* I had three of the steel darts tipped with a special poison developed by Harold D. It was like saxitoxin, only this poison was from the anal fin of the scorpion fish. Shoot a man on the beach, he dies in agony—but seemingly by accident. Oops, didn't watch where he was putting his feet. Must have stepped on one of those ugly and deadly little fish. More than one Soviet agent around the world had died "accidentally" thanks to Harold D.

But Jason refused the deadly darts. He said he didn't trust himself and, besides, if it came down to it, he had his knife.

And I had my knife, too. My lucky knife: the Randall attack-survival Model 18. It was seven and a half inches of the finest stainless-steel blade with a compartment in the hilt made waterproof by a threaded brass butt cap sealed with an O-ring. It had seen me through plenty of tough times. And had saved my life more than once. Just as a precaution, I unscrewed the cap and slid one of the little poisonous darts into the handle.

Just in case.

Rain came down in a slanting blaze of wind and lightning. Seas were a heaving green, waves four to six feet. One hell of a storm. Seas could be worse. But the rain couldn't.

"Maybe we shouldn't have left the Whaler behind," I yelled above the wind.

"We'll be okay in this. I thought you SEALs grew up in inflatables!"

We dropped it over the side, and it surged against *Sniper* in the waves. One thing forever good about inflatables—once you reach your destination, you can hide it with a couple of slices of the knife. We would paddle it the half mile down to the *Libertad*, sink it, then swim the rest of the way. I had on my camouflaged BC vest and my dark-blue Navy watch sweater and cap, and I wore my wrist compass. Jason wanted a tank. I didn't. I already had the Cobra crossbow with the blunted knockout tips strapped to my back.

And I don't like to be hampered.

The first surprise we got was when we neared the *Libertad*. There wasn't just one boat, there were three: the Cuban shrimp boat had anchored a few hundred yards away from it, and the white skiff we had seen leaving through the storm had been tied off the stern on a long line.

"What do you think, Captain?"

Jason kept paddling on. "We might be in over our heads is what I think."

"Wayne was in over his head when they got their hands on him, too. I say you take the shrimp boat and I'll take the barge. Signal me with your flashlight when you have the area secured."

"Aye-aye!"

Fifty yards from the barge, I slit the raft, letting it sink beneath us. Jason disappeared under the night sea, regulator in his mouth. I battled through the storm breathing through my snorkel, propelling myself along with the good TX-1000 Competition Class fins. When I got to the stern of the barge I held on to the diver's platform, resting.

Out of shape. Out of wind. And not very damn smart.

I should have known then.

A white flash of lightning brought the name of the barge in pulsing black: *Libertad, Miami, Fla.*

And I wondered how Castro had slipped them in on us. Not that hard, really. Send them across the Straits in a ratty boat and let them pretend to be refugees. Finance them, instruct them, let them train on American soil under the guise of being anti-Castro forces.

Easy enough.

And only possible in America.

I pulled the crossbow from off my shoulder. I armed it with a shaft and slid back the automatic cocking device. Some weapon. I had never been without it in Nam. It's made of light alloy with a draw weight of 150 pounds. The arrows were D. Harold's invention. If you just wanted to knock out a sentry, you used the blunt blade guards and shot him almost anywhere in the cranium area. If you wanted to kill, you pulled the blunt tips off.

The crossbow is another of the good things technology has all but left behind. It's silent. It has a stopping power equivalent to a full-load .45 slug and it's deadly.

The first guard was waiting for me. He was hidden behind an oil drum. When I pulled myself up onto the deck, I should have realized. Like in the westerns: It was quiet. Too quiet. Emanuel Ortiz was far too efficient to leave his vessel unguarded—especially after my earlier visit.

He had a knife. I saw him coming at me in a burst of lightning. Stocky guy in a rain slicker. He held the knife high and jumped at me. From behind. One thing saved me.

My mask. He tried to stab me in the right eye. I saw it coming and held up my hands in a feeble attempt to stop him. My mask was pushed up on my forehead. The point of the knife caught the bottom part of the mask, busting through the shatterproof glass, then cut across forehead bone, grating.

In the strange, slow-motion rush of the moment, I thought oddly:

Great. Another goddamn scar.

He wanted to play rough. No scare tactics this time. No more make-believe sharks to shoot at.

And that was fine with me. With one thrust of his knife, the stocky Cuban had outlined a whole new set of rules in my mind. Jason could try to be the gentle conqueror if he wanted. But they had murdered Wayne and probably Gifford, and now they were trying to kill me.

It was time to take off the gloves.

My Cobra crossbow clattered to the deck when the knife hit me. I grabbed the Cuban's elbow, lifted up and twisted, then hit him full-fisted under the armpit, right in the heart. He *oomphed* loudly and started to sag. I clamped onto the hand which held the knife, pulled it toward me, leveled the blade, then jammed it back into his own right eye, point first. He squirmed in death as I dropped him down on the storm-slick deck.

"Hold it!"

A dark figure stood before the wheelhouse cabin, crouching in the rain. He held a weapon I knew well: the Russian AK-47. It might even have been mine.

I made a motion to hold up my hands, then in one swift belly slide, I dove for the crossbow, hearing a burst of slugs splinter the deck behind me, following me along. As I rolled, I flipped the blunt tip from the shaft and fired. Quick shot, one-handed. I wanted to hit him in the heart. I missed.

Fffftt-THUD.

He dropped his weapon, clawing at something. A flare of lightning showed me.

The arrow had gone through his throat, nailing him against the cabin wall. He hung there grotesquely, pulling at the shaft. I could hear the rasp of air escaping from the hole in his windpipe.

Lights came on in the cabin. Shouts in wild Spanish. I picked up the assault rifle and retrieved my shaft. He fell onto the hatchway with a hollow thud. Through the cabin window, I could see four or five Cubans getting weapons from an aluminum locker. Ortiz wasn't among them.

I wondered how Jason was doing. It was too late for reason. For us to get away safely, we'd have to eliminate or capture them all. If not, those kids would be like sitting ducks on Fullmoon Cay. They had no radio, no idea what in the hell was going on. I reached over with the rifle and tapped on the door. I wanted them outside. One of them, the guy who had shot into the water with his sidearm earlier, looked up and saw me through the window. The automatic in his hands roared, throwing glass and wood all over me. I felt the blood from my knife wound drip hotly down my face, diluted by the rain.

I crawled along the cabin wall, then pulled myself up onto the roof.

They came spilling out of the cabin in a burst of fire. They mistook one of their fallen comrades for me, and loaded him up with lead. The body went sliding across the deck like an empty cup at a midnight fairgrounds. I watched from above, flat on my stomach. One of the Cubans moved around the starboard walkway, toward the bow. On the foredeck, he nosed around stacks of barrels and equipment, then stood up, perplexed. I took him cleanly with a shaft through the heart. He tumbled over backward into the water, the splash lost in the noise of the storm.

"MacMorgan!" one of them yelled in bad English. "Give yourself up. We will not kill you, *amigo*—honestly!"

One of them finally got the idea to look on top of the cabin. He came crawling up by himself, head swerving this way and that. I grabbed him by the hair from the side and shoved my knife deep into his brain, through the ear.

"MacMorgan! It is hopeless!"

It was hopeless, all right. For them. There were only two left. They had taken cover on the stern. When I didn't answer, they opened fire. But their angle was bad. I felt the popping vacuum of slugs passing over me. I slid backward on my belly, past the big chrome searchlight and horn, and dropped down into the foredeck.

From the side of the cabin I had a clear shot at them. It was assault-rifle time. I didn't mind drawing the fire of just two weapons. Besides, they wouldn't have long to shoot back.

Shooting a human being with a high-caliber automatic is a strange feeling. The way their bodies jolt and jump, it is as if you are connected to them by some high-voltage cord of electricity. I didn't make them jump long.

It didn't take much.

From the cabin, I heard some anxious voice hailing the *Libertad* on the VHF. It was in Spanish, and I recognized the voice: Emanuel Ortiz. Probably on the shrimp boat a few hundred yards away. It was bad news, hearing him. It could only mean one thing. They had gotten Jason. The gentle giant. The religion he had loved so well had gotten him killed or captured.

No, certainly killed. They would take no prisoners after what I had done.

I listened closely to what Ortiz was saying, and finally realized that he was demanding to know if I had been "taken care of."

I picked up the mike, pressed the button, and forced myself to cackle as if a part of some great conspiracy. *"Señor MacMorgan es muy enfirmo!"* I said it in a loud, raspy voice. When Ortiz began demanding more information, I switched the set off. I was very sick all right. I was damn sick of my friends' being killed without explanation. Why in the hell had Castro sent them? What were they doing posing as treasure hunters?

I grabbed a fresh crescent-shaped clip for the AK-47 from the aluminum locker, then threw the rest of the weapons overboard. With the assault rifle over one shoulder and the crossbow over the other, I slid back into the water and headed for the big shrimp boat, *Jose Martí*.

The deck was deserted. Wind blew the rain off the rails and blurred the bright cabin windows. But I had seen that kind of emptiness earlier, so I pulled myself up onto the boat very, very carefully.

Nothing. No one alive or dead.

I could hear voices from inside the cabin. I pulled my fins off and crawled across the deck. Ever so slowly, I lifted an eye to a porthole. A chill went through me. They had Jason. He sat at a table with Emanuel Ortiz. The tall Arabic-looking guy stood over him. Other Cubans drank coffee from tiny cups. Their weapons were leaned against the cabin wall.

I had no choice. There was only one thing I could do. I took the Cobra from off my shoulder and put it down on the deck. I made sure the assault rifle was still on automatic. I ducked under the glow of windows, and went to the cabin door. And with a deep breath, I kicked the door open and jumped through, ready to fire.

But I didn't.

It was too little too late.

Emanuel Ortiz smiled at me. He looked like a rat. He held a revolver to Jason's head. He was confident that he had me. And he was right.

"Drop your weapon, Captain MacMorgan. That's right, the knife, too. Now kick them away."

When I had done it, he put his gun down on the table within easy reach of Jason. And I knew then that if he could be so stupid we still had a chance. He started laughing. Softly at first. Then louder. He laughed the way an adult laughs at a silly child. "You were right about him, Mr. Boone. Absolutely correct. He is a tough man to kill, and he is absolutely dependable in—how did you put it?—his unflinching sense of duty? But you've troubled us for the last time, Captain."

And then I watched dumbfounded as Jason reached over and picked up the revolver. His eyes were strange, like those of some prophet who hears only one voice. He aimed the gun at me, and his hands were steady. "This would have been a lot easier, Dusky, if they had killed you out there." He gave the odd low whistle that I had heard before, and the beautiful redhead, Jennifer, came through the door. She carried a coil of rope and stopped at stern attention beside Jason.

"Dusky, I'm afraid I'm going to have to let this tall fellow here knock you out for a while. As a professional, I think you'll appreciate the skill with which he will do it. He's a martial-arts expert now studying the . . . ah . . . methods of the Castro regime." Jason looked up at the man. He had a gray complexion and the obligatory mustache and a coarse black beard. "Iranian, aren't you?"

The man nodded. And then he came toward me, smiling, relaxed. He held out his hand as if to shake mine. I saw it coming, but I couldn't block it. He was too fast. He jumped, swung, and the heel of his left leg caught me right behind the left ear. Stars and circles time. Felt like it took forever to fall. And through the pain, and bright colors, I heard Jason tell Jennifer that he would have to ask God what to do with me, and I hit the cabin deck, the question still formed on my lips.

Why . . . ?

17

Sound of an engine. Darkness and the roll of sea. I was in some kind of dark hold. I lay on a bunk. Mattress, no sheet. It smelled musty, and I could hear footsteps outside the darkness. Exchange of voices—man and a woman. A door opened, and in the quick brightness I could see the Iranian, outside.

So he was my guard.

The door shut and a light came on. It was Jennifer. She held a bowl in her hands and I could smell the warm odor of broth. She came over and sat on the bunk.

"So. You're awake."

"What in the hell does Jason think he's doing, Jennifer? He's crazy, you know. He's got to be."

She pushed me back down when I tried to sit up. She looked at me sternly and clicked her tongue in disapproval. "You musn't swear around me again, Dusky. I don't like it. And Jason is *not* crazy. He brought me to Jesus. He's showing us all the way." She began spooning out the broth to me.

"And was it Jason who killed Wayne? Remember Wayne, Jennifer—the guy you said you loved?''

"I didn't say I loved him. I just said I wanted his babies.'' She thought for a moment. Such a pretty face and such dead, dead eyes. "And no, Jason didn't kill Wayne. Jason hasn't killed anyone, Dusky. Sometimes he asks us to, but it is always the will of God. It was their time.''

"And what if your time comes, Jennifer?''

"Then it's His will.''

She put the bowl down and began cleaning my face with a cloth. She said, "You know, I felt so very bad when Wayne was taken.'' She sighed. There was a faraway look in her eyes. "He was so strong and . . . good.''

I reached out and shook her gently by the shoulders. "You're right, Jennifer, he *was* good. Listen to me, Jennifer! Think about what I'm saying. Wayne *was* good, but they killed him anyway . . .''

Her eyes started to water, and then, as I continued, she started sobbing, tears rolling down her cheeks. "No, no. Wayne wouldn't join us. He wouldn't join Jesus. When Jason finally told him about our work, Wayne got very upset. He wanted to go tell you. He had to be sent out here, he had to be . . . it was His will . . .''

"You loved him, Jennifer.''

"No!''

"Get me a gun and help me.''

"I *didn't* love him. I just wanted his baby. I wanted your baby when they . . . when they took him away. Jason told me you were as suitable . . .'' She was sobbing wildly now. The door opened and my guard stuck his head in.

"Do you need some assistance?" He spoke very careful, very proper English in that irritating manner of the wellborn Mediterranean.

"Get your ass out of here, buddy!"

He leaned against the doorjamb and sneered. "You Americans," he said. "You speak with such force and yet are so soft."

Jennifer moved quickly between us, wiping her eyes. "No," she said. "You musn't, Isfahan. Not until Jason says." She stopped and looked at me before going out the door. "You are wrong about us, Dusky. Ours is the only way."

She closed the door and I was in darkness again.

When the engines hit reverse, jolting, and I heard the chain-rasp and splash of the anchor, I sat up, wondering where we were, what we were doing. It made no sense. Nothing made any sense. I went to the door and pounded on it.

"What is it?" It was the Iranian, Isfahan.

"Tell Jason I want to talk with him. It's important."

"All in good time. In good time."

It crossed my mind that I might be able to bait him, to bring him charging in. "Don't give me that 'good time' crap, you flunky bastard. I'm ordering you—get him now!"

He only chuckled softly, and I sat back down, feeling like a fool. In the darkness I groped around trying to find a weapon, any kind of weapon. Nothing. I knew what it was like to be blind. I lifted the mattress up hoping to find a loose brace. I traced the hull planking, wondering if one might be loose. In one of the planks, there was some kind of rough-cut design pressed into the wood.

Letters. Two letters, I ran my fingers over them, Braille-like.

W. P.

Wayne Peters.

So they had had him on the shrimp boat all along. I wondered if he had heard me on the morning that I stopped. No, he would have called to me. The Iranian must have worked him over. But somehow he had escaped, made it to the boat, and then . . . the bomb. But how would they know to plant it there? And then I knew. They had expected me to take the boat. Jason had tipped them off. Instead of radioing the Coast Guard, he had radioed the Cubans.

I searched myself for anger, and found none. Not for Jason, anyway. It surprised me. I felt only pity. I had been in the same jungles and seen the same horrors. And I had seen men, good men like Jason, snap. They had hurt him over there, in mind and body. It was easy to guess the kind of wound which made it impossible for him to ever have children. So he had turned to God and, in his own mind, become God. In his brilliance, he had put together some sort of strange religious organization. Radio, television; millions of Americans, probably, tuning in and supporting the work of his Christ's Children of America. And surrounding him, he kept a small group of the cult-stricken; the brightest and the best of those who fell in his spell. Wayne Peters wouldn't give in, though. He was too strong. So he had been eliminated, murdered when Jason had told him of the group's "real work."

But what was that work?

I didn't have to wait long to find out.

The light came on, and Jason Boone came quietly through the door. He wore a red foul-weather jacket and the same black stocking cap he had worn on our "mission." The strangeness was still in his eyes, but he seemed nervous, almost embarrassed by the situation. He kept folding and unfolding his big hands, and his head shook with a slight pathological tremor. He sat down beside me on the bunk.

"Jason."

"Yes, Dusky."

"You're insane, Jason. You know that, don't you?"

He didn't even flush. "No, you're wrong. I'm not. God has told me what I must do. It's not always easy, Dusky, but I'm not insane. I would feel much better if you believed me."

"Why didn't you kill me yourself? Last night? It would have been easier on both of us."

He looked at me as if surprised I could even think such a thing. "Dusky, I couldn't kill you. If I could have, I would have killed you the night we came onto your boat. I couldn't ask Wayne because he didn't know of our work. I had to ask one of my other children, but he couldn't kill you either. You were too strong for him. I'm sorry he cut your face."

"But you could kill Wayne? How could you do that?"

He shook his head quickly. "No!" He almost yelled it. And then the soft, searching voice returned. "No, I didn't want Wayne killed. That would be insane. Wayne was . . . perfect. I wanted

him to have it all, Dusky. I wanted him to mate
with our most perfect woman; to bear a child. The
others are my children, Dusky. He was to be my
son. But he wouldn't listen. He just wouldn't.
When I told him of my work, my plans, he got
very upset. I told him that night after the supper
on the beach. We were alone in the boat. He demanded that I take him to see you. I couldn't do
that, Dusky. I had to take him out to this shrimp
boat so he could think things over. But he struggled with Isfahan. Isfahan hurt him very badly,
but Wayne still got away. I didn't know what had
happened until you told me. He was my son,
Dusky, but it was God's will. He had to die as . . .
as an example to the others, I guess. He died for
them all." Jason put his face in his hands, breathing deeply. "When I came back to the island that
night, I found Buster Ronstadz snooping around.
He told me he had watched me go to the Cuban
boat, and he threatened to tell the police I was
dealing in drugs if I didn't help put him on the
wreck he was searching for. We will have nothing
to do with drugs, but I couldn't take the chance
of getting the police involved. I was upset from
my talk with Wayne. Ronstadz made me very
angry. He was a Judas and deserved to die. He
wanted to interfere with my mission."

"And just what is your mission, Jason? And just
what in the hell does it have to do with these
Castro goons?"

"Our past lives were so similar, I thought you
would have guessed."

"I tried but didn't like what I came up with."

"God has told me to save our race, Dusky. The

dark ones are taking over the world." He pointed to his groin, and his nostrils flared slightly. "A slopehead did this to me! And now they're trying to take over our country. Can't you see it, Dusky? After I was wounded, I lay for months in the hospital. I read the papers, studied national social and political trends. I'm a student of history, Dusky! I saw what few others can see. There has never been a war in the history of man that wasn't directly or indirectly racially motivated. The Celts, the Romans, the Germans, the Japanese—yes, and even the Vietnamese. All of them. And now, for the first time in our country's history, the dark ones are threatening to outnumber us. Read the papers! They are crushing us with their demands for welfare, and they destroy our cities with their filth and their crimes and their riots. The next great war isn't going to be with atomic weapons, Dusky, it's going to be us against them with small arms. It's going to be won or lost in the cities, on the streets. And my people are going to be ready!"

"I guess you never saw any of the good, brave blacks in Nam . . ."

"I'm not just talking about blacks."

"Jason! Jason, listen to me. Do you realize you sound like Hitler?"

He stood up and smacked his hand with a big fist. "Hitler was right! Why do you think I made my home base in Davenport? It's the center for the American Nazi Party. They're helping me prepare . . ."

His voice wavered a little when he said it. His eyes were worried, haunted. "I could never kill innocent women and children—not like them. When the war does come, I couldn't allow it to be that way. No, of course we won't. God will tell us what to do. And by that time, my children will be ready. They are seeding the new race now; the best and the brightest young people I could find. And they're keeping their genes pure. Don't you see, Dusky? We're *using* the communists! I made my contact with Emanuel Ortiz in the VA hospital. He's a physical therapist. We talked a lot. He thought I hated America; he made it known that he might be able to help me—but he doesn't know why. He thinks I'm a commie, too. And anyone but the fools at the State Department can see why Castro planted his group here—to aid people like me! I give them gold, and they give me weapons. Finding the treasure is no problem. My missionaries in Europe, along with being good Christians, are also the best-educated, most-dedicated researchers to have ever gone through the archives in Madrid."

"So why did you come to my boat looking for that gold chain, if it's so easy to find?"

"I didn't want the chain. I thought you might have a chart showing where the main lode of the *Gaspar* was located. I'm afraid when Detective Herrera asked me about Gifford Remus, he told me the whole story. We've made it possible for the Cubans to find enough treasure to keep them interested, but if I could find the *Gaspar*—well, we could buy enough arms for everyone in our movement."

"You didn't kill Remus?"

He shook his head. "I have no idea who did."

"My people told me this shrimp boat had been searched. Where do you keep the treasure and the weapons? How do you make the switch?"

"The shrimp boat is moved to deep water. It makes rendezvous with a Cuban submarine. Emanuel does the actual salvage. I just put him on the wrecks. One of our connections in Davenport has a small fleet of shrimp boats in Texas. When we're done here, one of the boats will be properly manned and sent down to pick up the weapons. We were keeping them on Emanuel's barge. But my people are transferring them to our camp now, burying them on Fullmoon Cay in waterproof containers. You should see them work, Dusky! They're happy! They have a common goal, a common cause, and faith in the mission God has given us." He stopped, thoughtful for a moment. He put his hand on my shoulder gently. "Join us, Dusky. Wayne is gone. Jennifer will be yours. I was so hoping that when she came to you that night, you would. Your child would be a great blessing to us . . ."

"I could lie to you, Jason, and tell you I don't think you're crazy. I could lie to you and tell you that I believe."

His bright-blue eyes looked deeply into mine. "No, Dusky. You could never do that."

"Jason, you know that you need help. Think back, Jason. Think back to Nam. You saw them snap. Remember the way we joked about them? We joked because, deep inside, we knew it could happen to us. And it scared us. And now it's happened to you . . ."

He stood up abruptly, rubbing his hands together as if to clean them. He said, "You know that the only thing that is keeping you alive now is Ortiz. He thinks you know where the *Gaspar* is. I told him that so I would have a chance to talk with you. To give you a chance. When you tell them you don't know, they'll let Isfahan try to beat it out of you. After that, if you're not already dead, they'll kill you."

"You're playing right into their hands, you know. The Cubans, the communists—they're the true enemies, Jason. And you're helping these people. Once you've shown them all the treasure you can find, they're going to take their weapons and—"

He held up his hand. "They're a stupid, greedy, and godless people, Dusky. Remember how the slopes were? It is true that they think they are using me. But that's not the way it is. When the submarine comes to make the final pickup, they will try to demand their weapons back. But I'm ready for them. Like all the dark ones, they are a stupid people. I have made certain deliveries to each of their boats. As an explosives expert yourself, you can understand what I am saying. I have but to push a button on my boat. And I will. When the time is right."

I said nothing. He opened the door to go, then turned to me with the sad, sad eyes. He looked like the haunted brother from another lifetime.

"They'll come for you tonight, Captain, when the rest of us are asleep. Isfahan is a master with his feet. It is the only way he could have possibly hurt Wayne." He hesitated. "Good luck, Dusky. I'll . . . pray for you . . ."

18

Jason was right. They came for me in the darkness. First Emanuel Ortiz. He made me lie on my belly with my hands behind me while we talked. He carried a revolver. Ortiz was not one to take chances. At first he was pleasant. He made small jokes. He wanted me to tell him where the *Gaspar* was.

"We searched your boat, Mr. MacMorgan. The gold chain wasn't that well hidden. Mr. Boone tells me the chain was described in detail in the manifest of the *Gaspar* his researchers found in the Madrid archives."

"Jason Boone is insane, Ortiz."

He laughed shortly. "Of course he is. He's a product of your capitalistic system. Those who are not physically weak are mentally corrupt. It is sad but true."

"I had forgotten—Comrade Stalin forbade your system to acknowledge your sick and infirm. I've always wondered, Ortiz—after Castro executes them, does he just bury them, or does he have them ground up for food to feed your starving?"

He was silent for a moment. I could feel the hatred in him.

"I'm becoming impatient with your stupidity, gringo. Tell us where the *Gaspar* is, and I will spare your life."

"I don't know where it is, Ortiz."

"I think it is very clear that you do, and—"

"The last time you thought clearly, Ortiz, is the last time you sat down to piss."

I heard him get to his feet. He said, "I believe you have met our Iranian friend, Isfahan? He is one of our comrades. And we have many like him around the world. We are united, gringo. We are smarter and stronger, and living in your country these past years has demonstrated just how easy it will be when the time comes. Perhaps I should send Isfahan in to speak with you? He will hurt you, MacMorgan, and then, if you still refuse to talk, he will kill you. With his bare hands."

"Ortiz?"

"Yes."

"The only way that Iranian grease slick of yours could beat me in a fight is to cut my head off— and then hide it from me."

It worked. He was raging. He sputtered as he talked.

"You American fool! You have the audacity . . . he has already beaten you once! And you still insist . . . So be it! You will have your meeting with Isfahan! And when it is over, we will throw your body to the fish!"

He went out and slammed the door behind him. I heard their voices faintly. Ortiz was still angry, yelling. While I waited, I tried to formulate a plan. I didn't have much to work with. But I had to use what I had. It was my only slim chance.

When the Iranian came through into the hold he had a wry smile on his face. I heard the sound of the door being locked behind him.

"You have upset my Cuban comrade, Yankee."

"Gee, I'm sorry as hell, Isfa-*fool*."

He started to correct me, then caught himself. He forced himself to smile again. "It will not work with me, Yankee. But before we are finished with our meeting perhaps I can persuade you to say my name correctly."

We stood just about eye to eye. He might have had an inch on me. He was corded, sinewy; all grace and self-assurance. The look in his eyes belied the smile. They were the same color as his short coarse beard, and they were filled with hatred. And what did I have on him—fifteen pounds? Yeah, fifteen pounds and probably ten years.

I was ready for the first kick, but he still got me. He feinted to the left, then caught me with a whirling, glancing blow behind the ear. He wanted to finish it fast. But I blocked just enough of it to keep my feet. He was quick. Too damn quick. I glanced up at the ceiling at the lightbulb. It was sealed in with wire. Perhaps I should just knock it out now and take my chances with the Iranian in the dark.

No, he would call for the guards. And it wasn't part of my plan.

He threw a series of low quick kicks at me, then nailed me right under the chin. I could feel my jaw grate as I moved my mouth. It had knocked me backward onto the bunk.

"Perhaps you would like to try my name again, Yankee?" There was no smile now. He wasn't even breathing heavily. I had to somehow get in close on him, but how? If Wayne, an All-American wrestler, couldn't do it, how would I?

I got shakily to my feet. I had to lure him into a mistake; make him hesitate in the process of taking me apart with his feet. I said:

"Do you know what I like about you Iranians?"

He looked momentarily surprised. "No, Yankee. What is that?"

"Not a goddam thing, Isfa-*fool*. Not a goddam thing."

He started to come at me. I held up my hands, then reached slowly into my pocket and took out my tin of snuff. Watching him carefully, I took a big pinch, then held out the can toward him.

"Like a little taste before I kill you?"

His mouth became an ugly slit within his beard. "You silly American fool!" He jumped and kicked the can out of my hand. The silver lid caromed around the room.

"Buddy," I said, "you've just really pissed me off."

He made his mistake. The one I had been praying for. He came at me with a twisting flurry of kicks, and then tried to use his hands on me. I ducked under and caught one of the wrists, holding him with my arm around his stomach. I had spent my entire boyhood in the circus gripping a

trapeze bar. I knew how to grip. I squeezed until
the sweat came; I squeezed until I heard the thin
radius and ulna bones pop. He gave a soft low
squeal, then put me on my knees with a back kick
to the groin. A direct hit. I fought back the nausea,
trying to fend off his kicks at my face. I took a
solid shot to the ribs and felt some bones go. I
waited for him, knowing what he would do. He
leaned over me then, his one good hand folded
like an ax, and took a swing at my throat. I caught
it, twisted, and nailed him with a Copenhagen
stinger right in the eyes. He gave another squeal,
rubbing at his face. By that time, I was on my feet.
I hit him with a straight overhand that split his
mustache up to his eye, then swung him around
to the bunk and sat him down, my hand on his
windpipe.

"Listen to me, asshole . . ."

He tried to struggle, and I gripped down on his
Adam's apple.

"*Listen!* You do exactly as I say, and I'll spare
you. When I give you the word, I want you to
shout to the guards. Tell them I'm dead and to let
you out."

"How do I know I can trust you?" he hissed.
He was scared, ready to bargain.

"Let's just say that you can bet your life on it."

He nodded. I pulled his shoe off, reached up,
and knocked the ceiling light out on my third
swing. I stood him up, my hand still at his throat.

"*Now!*"

He yelled it, and he yelled it loud. And the moment the words were out of his mouth, I jerked

his windpipe loose, and he went fluttering around the room like a dying balloon.

Guess what, asshole . . . I lied . . .

By the time the guards got the door open, I was ready and waiting. There were a lot of voices: fast, enthusiastic Spanish. They must have been listening from outside, maybe even betting on the fight. The first guard came in, squinting into the darkness. I grabbed the assault rifle from his hands, dented his face with the barrel, then opened fire. There were four or five of them, and they went down wide-eyed, horrified, trying to ready their own weapons. They were shocked. The American had won. They were shocked to death.

I gave them another sweeping burst, and saw the ass-end of Emanuel Ortiz disappear up the steps, onto the deck. And like an idiot, I charged after him.

He stood flat against the outside cabin wall, waiting. When he knocked the rifle from my hands, I stumbled and heard his pistol explode above my ear. I made a blind grab for his hand and fell into him, punching wildly at his face. I heard other voices as I finally connected with Emanuel's jaw. There were more of them; more Castro Cubans. Without looking back, I made a headlong dive into the water. There was the moist *pop-a-pop-a-pop* of automatic weapons behind me, and I dove.

Dive deep, MacMorgan. Dive and swim until the broken ribs throb and your lungs are ready to burst. Push yourself until it's impossible to go any farther,

*because they're up there waiting, and you used up all
your luck a long, long time ago.*

They didn't expect me to surface seventy-five
yards away. When the searchlight finally found
me, their shots were wild and low. Rough breaking seas and a wild storm moon. Some night for
a swim. They had another searchlight trained on
Sniper. They had brought her back to Fullmoon
Cay, and she heaved on her anchor line. They expected me to swim to that blue haven, and that's
exactly why I couldn't.

The slugs were smacking into the big waves,
closer to me now. I dove again, heading for the
island.

Pull, frog-kick, glide.

When I came up again, the searchlight tunneled
crazily in the darkness, sweeping back and forth.
They had lost me. I heard them start up one of
the skiffs. Search-party time. I gulped down the
heavy storm air, testing my ribs with a swollen
hand. The Iranian bastard had definitely busted
a couple.

But he had paid a damn high price for them.

I dove again, heading toward the surf which
crashed up on the darkness of the jungled beach,
away from the camp. And with a final last breath,
I let the sea throw me onto the cold sand.

I knelt on the beach, my head turning. One of
the skiffs had landed, and men scurried in the
moonlight, far down the island. They were onto
my little game.

The last thing I heard before disappearing into
the mangrove swamp was the voice of Jason call-

ing to his group. I had escaped, and he wanted them to all join in the search.

I could hear Christ's Children in the darkness. They were all around me, moving across the island in a web of humanity. I heard the low voice of the lithe blonde a few yards away, and remembered her strange song:

> Come with Him,
> He has chosen us,
> To win our peace
> The chosen must . . .

The poor mixed-up kids. I felt sorry for them all. It was easy to see how it had happened. The cult groups were filled with them: the lost ones, rich and poor, looking for goals, a cause. They wanted only hope and a reason to follow. They wanted a God who would answer all the questions that have never truly been answered; they yearned for a leader to show them the way.

This way.

That way.

Any way . . .

I had climbed to the top of a big gumbo-limbo tree, hiding myself in the foliage. Clouds streamed by overhead, and I could hear the pounding sea. They were headed across the island, in the darkness toward the other side. Fine. Good. That's where I *wanted* them to go.

And when they had passed, I swung painfully down. My only hope was to get to a boat. Or at least get to a VHF and tell the Coast Guard just what in the hell was going on before they killed me.

I made my way through the night, one careful step at a time. This was my game now; this was what I had been trained for. Slide from shadow to shadow. Test every bit of footing. You never know where someone might be waiting. In the jungle, in the night, the anxious and the hasty end up very, very dead.

The camp seemed empty when I finally crept out of the darkness onto the beach. I had sat in the brush and watched it for a long time. From the other side of the island I could hear shouts, and the occasional *pop* of gunfire. I wondered who they were shooting at. I wondered who they were killing.

Themselves, probably.

There were no lights on aboard *Sniper*. But in the moonlight I saw a sudden shadowed move, and I knew that they had guards on it. Both the *Jose Martí* and the *Superior* were brightly lighted. But there was still my little Whaler. I knew where it had to be—and it was: fifty yards offshore, within easy range of anyone shooting from the shrimp boat. It was just beyond the camp, across the beach. And I had to try for it.

I had no choice.

When you have to abandon your cover and move across a clearing, you can't allow yourself to rush. You can't act like the hunted, or they know. When there is only enough light for shadows and silhouettes, you have to act as if you're one of them, and do it as if your life depends upon it—because it does.

I stepped casually onto the beach, my hands in my pockets. I walked slowly but surely toward the surf. Passed one tent. Passed another. And just as I was about ready to disappear into the water, I heard a voice.

"Hello, Dusky."

It was Jason. He sat inside the last tent, holding a revolver.

I turned slowly, my hands up.

"Hello, Jason."

He got to his feet, brushing off the sand. He moved a little closer to me, but not too close. I could see his face plainly in the moonlight.

"I knew what you would do, Dusky. I tried to tell Emanuel, but he wouldn't listen."

I should have realized earlier that it was true. I could fool the rest of them, but not Jason. Not a Green Beret.

I shrugged. "The surest means of escape . . ."

". . . is through the enemy's camp," he finished softly. There was a strange emptiness in his voice; the same great sadness in his eyes. He looked like a pathetic big kid who hears voices no one else can hear. He leveled the gun at my face, and I heard the double *click* of the hammer. "I have no choice, Dusky. I can't let you go. You would ruin . . . ruin my mission." He stopped, tilting his head, listening again. And then: "Besides, you wouldn't have a chance anyway. Emanuel and his men would follow you in my boat. It's faster. If the sea was calmer, your Whaler could outrun them—but not when it's like this. They'd run you down and kill you anyway. And then they would wonder why I hadn't."

I heard a thin little whimper from within the tent. It was Jennifer. She came crawling out, wiping her eyes. She said, "Jason . . . Jason, please give us a chance. We won't say a word—not to anyone. Honest."

Jason looked at me. "You talked to her out there on the shrimp boat, Dusky. You made her doubt. That's not good, Dusky. We can't afford a loss of faith among my children. You and Wayne are too much alike, Dusky. You make people doubt . . . even my own son . . ."

From the island came the flat, distant sound of gunfire.

"You know what's happening in there, don't you, Jason?"

He made a helpless motion with his hand. "I told them not to shoot unless they were absolutely sure, but . . ." He stopped and looked at me. "But they're not like us, Dusky. They don't know how it is. They don't know how it is in the jungle at night, when you can smell the . . . smell the flesh . . . the awful, burning flesh . . ."

He cocked his head, listening. It was as if he heard a voice too far in the distance to understand. In the moonlight, his beard was a flowing crimson. Jennifer burst into tears and came running into my arms. I stroked her hair. Down the beach, I saw a boat land. One of the little skiffs. The Castro Cubans jumped out and started running toward us.

"They're coming, Jason."

"Yes, I see them." His head tilted, straining to listen. "Wayne . . . I killed him, Dusky. In my own way, I killed my own—"

"Jason, back in Nam! In the jungle! We were all hurt . . . but you were the best, and you were hurt the worst. But it's not too late. That voice you hear, Jason, the voice you're hearing right now, is no stranger. It's a voice you haven't heard in a long time, Jason. Remember? It's the man you used to be before . . . before the jungle."

He shook himself. His eyes moved slowly from side to side like a man just coming out of a trance, unsure of where he was.

"It's not too late, Dusky, is it? Damn! It's *not*!"

"No, Captain. Come with us. We'll get help and come back for the rest of them."

He smiled slightly. His eyes suddenly looked clear; good. "I'll come later. I'll . . . get the rest and—"

The Castro Cubans opened fire then, the slugs throwing stripes in the sand with the trajectory of arrows. Jason shoved us roughly toward the water. "Get your ass in gear, MacMorgan!"

As I pulled the girl along behind, Jason made a diving roll and came up firing. One of Ortiz's people fell clutching his face. Another crawled toward the bushes holding his stomach. The rest took quick cover.

"Dusky! We can't just leave him there!" The girl was near hysterics. "They'll kill him, Dusky!"

"Not before he's killed most of them!" I jerked her roughly toward the water.

The last time I saw Jason Boone was after I had jammed the Whaler into gear and gone roaring off through the heavy swells. He was a dark bulky figure in the soft light of the beach. He had used his six shots and left the revolver behind. The Cubans had caught on. Five of them were black heaps in the night. The rest had sought the safety of the inner island. Jason was on his belly, crawling toward them. He disappeared into the jungle . . .

Jason Boone was right, of course. He had predicted exactly what was to happen. When Emanuel Ortiz realized that we were escaping in the Whaler, he loaded the few men he could find in the sleek steel-hulled *Superior*.

It was also true that we didn't have a chance.

On a flat day, the Whaler can do right at forty mph. But on the stormy night sea, with the wind out of the west northwest, I had to quarter into it. Seas were six to eight feet, and we would either swamp or pitchpole if I tried to open her up.

The *Superior* was about a half mile behind, but gaining. Its big heavy hull crushed the confronting seas, and her twin screws drove her on. Every now and then, looking back, I could see the moonlight on the huge wake she threw. Her searchlight swept back and forth over the water, hunting us.

The most obvious sanctuary for us was the shoalwater around the Marquesas. In foul seas, the shallows would be awash with surf—it would be as risky as it was obvious.

Maybe it was a little too obvious.

Maybe Emanuel Ortiz was so confident that we would head for shoalwater that he wasn't paying attention.

It was worth a try.

"Hold on, woman!" I yelled to Jennifer. She sat huddled next to me, soaked and shaking. She

braced herself with her hands white on the
wooden bench seat of the little fourteen-foot boat.
Some boat, the Boston Whaler. It will take any
weather, survive any sea. And it was about to get
the acid test.

I picked my wave, cut sharply to starboard, then
surfed momentarily before sliding down the back-
side of the wave, heading toward the Straits of
Florida. Another black wall of water came up behind us and threw us onward. It was dangerous
work. If I gave her too much throttle, the wave
would crest with us and pitchpole us end over
end. If I gave her too little, the stern sea would
shove us sideways and cause us to broach.

"Keep an eye on that boat! If he starts to follow
us, let me know!"

I kept at it: five minutes, ten minutes.

"Dusky!"

"Yeah!"

"They've turned! They know where we are!"
She wasn't crying now. She was scared. Damn
scared. And so was I. I was just hoping that I hid
it as well as she did. The game was over. Emanuel
had been paying attention.

They had us on radar.

My little gamble had cost us precious time. And
we didn't have any to spare. I cut back to the
north and east, headed for the dark grace of the
Marquesas. It was winner-take-all time, and I
pushed the little Whaler as hard as she could possibly go, riding right on the edge of disaster. Every
breaker we quartered tossed us airborne, then let
us pound back into the trough with spine-
shattering impact. I winced with each assault, feel-

ing my broken ribs jab into my lungs. I felt weak. Sick. Beaten.

So this is it, MacMorgan. You knew the day would come. You knew the reaper would catch up and take you by the throat long before your contemporaries headed for their rest homes.

Yeah, but not because of a slimy Castro Cuban like Ortiz.

If he wanted me, he was going to have to work at it. What had he said?

You Americans—either mentally soft or physically weak.

We'd see.

We were about a mile and a half off the Marquesas. The islands looked strangely safe, strangely comforting, in the moonlight darkness. *Superior* was closing in fast, vectoring in on us like a heat-sensing missile. They had all their running lights on now. Ortiz and the few men he had left felt safe, secure. In control. They knew where I was and they were about to take their revenge.

Dammit, MacMorgan, think!

There was no way we could beat them to the shoalwaters of the island. We would somehow have to fight it out out here. My brain scanned wildly for options.

Jump and make a swim for it?

Not with the girl . . . No, she would have made it. She was the swimmer. I had to admit it to myself—I was the one who wouldn't have made it. Not with my ribs. I felt as if I was leaking blood, bleeding internally.

"Jump for it," I yelled to her. "Swim for the island! I'll lead them away—"

"I will do no such thing!"

The beam of the searchlight had found us now. It swept by, then jumped back, holding us. The *Superior* came booming onward.

"Do I have to throw your ass out of the boat, woman?"

"Dusky, I'm not leaving without you—"

I didn't hear the rest of what she said.

Because that's when I saw it.

A bright-orange buoy riding wildly in the sea ahead, caught in the shaft of searchlight. It marked something, and I knew exactly what.

I had put it there.

It was a long shot, but it was the only shot we had. I remembered the way they had looked on the bottom there: corroded half-globes, loosened by the current in the sweep of underwater river that plowed through the Navy's forbidden bombing and strafing area.

"Hang on, woman—and if you've still got it in you, give us a little prayer!"

I gunned the Whaler toward the orange buoy. They were shooting at us now, the sound of their weapons like dull thuds behind us. I made Jennifer lie flat on the deck.

Cut it close—as close as you can without fouling the prop. Make them follow, dammit!

They followed, all right—dead over the old field of magnetic mines.

It was a multiple explosion, the force so great that it singed my hair and almost blew us out of the boat. There were two dull, distant explosions, too—the shrimp boat and the salvage barge. Jason had set his charges well.

The steel hull of the *Superior* was in bright scattered flames, raining down on the water. And something else was raining down on us, too. Small. Heavy. Metallic. In the light of the fire, I picked one of the objects and studied it.

And suddenly I knew it all. I knew how Gifford Remus, my strange little friend, had died.

And I knew why no one had ever found the *Gaspar*.

The bottom of the Whaler was littered with gold doubloons . . .

19

It was one of those blustery December days. The kind that make the tourists wonder why they have left the cold of Ohio and New Jersey and paid all that money just to freeze their butts off in Florida. The wind roared icily out of the northwest, rolling a high stream of soot-colored clouds across the tropical skies, and palm trees, leaning in the gray wind, looked oddly out of place.

It should have been a day for being depressed; a bleak day for bleak soul-searching.

But it wasn't that way. Not with this woman. And besides, I was suddenly very rich.

Norm Fizer had come to visit me a month earlier in the hospital to give me the news.

"You scarred-up old bastard," he had said, smiling, mussing my hair as I lay in the sterile whiteness of sheets and chest brace. "The state permit we gave you as a cover is all of a sudden worth more than a winning ticket in the Irish Sweepstakes."

"Huh? Oh, that's nice, Norm."

"We sent some Navy divers out to disarm the rest of those mines and torpedoes, and they said the bottom is just covered with the stuff."

"What stuff, Norm?"

"Gold! Gold and silver and—"

"Hmm. That's nice."

"It's just a theory of mine, but I figure when the *Gaspar* went down, coral started to build around it. A little reef started. You know how those fighter pilots are—especially those World War Two flyboys. On a practice mission, any strange shape is fair game. They started loading it up with torpedoes and .30 caliber, and it became the natural place to anchor the old scow targets. When those went down and the war was over, the Navy declared the area off limits. Too many old unexploded bombs. It was the only safe place to dispose of their old mines."

"I'll be darned."

"So when the treasure hunters started nosing around out there, you can bet their magnetometers just went nuts when they passed over that area. But what did they see when they went down? Old bombs. A magnetometer can't tell the difference between gold and old iron, so they just got the hell away and didn't come back. Somehow that old man figured it out and started digging around. But he dug around one torpedo too many. Yes sir, Dusky old boy, you got money coming out the ears."

"What was that, Norm?"

He put his hands on his hips indignantly. "Hey, what's your problem, Captain? I stand here talking myself blue in the face, giving you great news, and you lie there like you've lost your best friend."

In a way, in a very strange way, I had.

Two of them.

First Wayne. And then Jason. Wayne had been a kindred spirit. He was the kind of guy I would have wanted my sons to be. And Jason . . . well, Jason was what the dark side of me could have become; what I had felt crawling around in my brain ratlike back in Nam. We were brothers of the same horrors, but polarized by . . . what?

Luck, I guess.

It happened to a lot of us, over there. In the jungle. If I had only been smart enough to see it in him earlier, and if I had only tried to get to him before . . .

If, if, if . . .

But Jason had realized too late. He had taken eight of them. The last three hand to hand. They found him dead, his hands around the throat of his final victim. He had been knifed in the stomach and chest and finally shot in the back.

But at least he had realized.

Surprisingly, none of his Christ's Children had been killed. Two had been slightly wounded, and all had been sent to special deprogramming facilities in Des Moines, where, apparently, they were all responding to treatment. Not surprising, really. As Jason had said, they were the best and the smartest.

But you can't let the dead pull you into the grave with them. As long as your heart beats, you have to find a way of going on. I had learned that all too well in the past.

"It's over," Norm has said, suddenly serious.

"Captain Boone was a good man."

"And there but for the grace of God . . . I know what you mean, Dusky."

"Norm," I said, "why don't you take a couple of weeks off? I'm going to get an old pirate I know by the name of Yarbrough. We'll go back to the Marquesas and all get rich."

He grinned. "I've got kids heading toward college age. I could use it."

"One thing, though. We each get ten percent. The rest will go to the veterans' hospitals around, and to a special little charity I have in mind."

"And the charity's initials are C.C.A., right? Sounds good. There were only those few who were in on Jason's . . . plan. I'm afraid we had to check them out pretty thoroughly. So it's a deal. Let's all go get wealthy."

So we did. Even April came out to join us for a while. I kept kidding her about the dream she had had.

"Well, dang it, part of it came true—you *were* in the hospital!"

It had been a pleasant time out there; the bad memories of the Marquesas and Fullmoon Cay coming only in the dark times; the lonely times when I slept alone on the flybridge, thinking. One night, April had come to me there. She didn't want romance. She wanted to talk. It was funny the way she started. Very frank, very businesslike. When the time came, she wanted to get married, and she wanted to get married to me.

"Impossible," I had told her.

And she had looked at me softly with her

golden eyes. "You mean . . . you mean you don't love me, Dusky?"

I felt the lie catch in my throat, but I forced it out. "No, April. No, I don't."

She watched my face carefully, saying nothing. And then she smiled. "You're a bad liar, MacMorgan."

"And you're pretty damn cocky, Miss Yarbrough!" I started to say something else, but she held up her hand.

"Let's just say we'll stay in touch, and leave it at that." She winked. "You're a man an' you're gonna have your friends, and I might even have some of mine. But when push comes to shove, MacMorgan, you know the way it's going to be with us. Someday."

And I had kissed her gently. "Okay, April. Someday."

So we had all returned to Key West rich. I contracted out the rest of the *Gaspar* to a group of professional salvage people on a percentage basis, and Hervey went back out with them to keep an eye on things. For the first time in my life, the figures in my bankbook were staggering. But money is both a blessing and a curse. It made me restless, nervous. So one day I went down to see a CPA friend of mine on Duval Street. I told him to stick almost all of my share into government bonds. Let the country use it to invest. And I didn't want to know what the figures were or the interest rate was, and I didn't want to see the income tax reports any longer than it took for me to sign them.

That done, I made a call to the Midwest. The woman seemed happy to hear from me.

Had the doctor helped her work out the problem?

Yes. Completely.

I was about to go on a little cruise. The real-estate people had given me a list of secluded waterfront and private island property around the Keys, and I wanted someone to go along with me and give me advice.

She would fly in within the week.

I knew there would be no shyness about her. There wasn't. When she wasn't wearing her sleek swimsuit, she was naked, lolling about oiled on the deck when it was warm enough. And when it wasn't warm enough, she was either puttering around, reading in the cabin, or oiled and ready, sleepy-eyed and wanting, beneath the covers of my bed.

It was a good week of cruising and cold beer and long, long love. We even found time to look at property. I had admitted to myself earlier that the *Sniper* was a perfect boat for fishing, but it just wasn't built to serve as a live-aboard for a guy my size. And I had to make a decision.

It came down to two places. The first was a private island—twenty acres of island. It had high shell mounds and a citrus grove, and a deepwater channel for dockage. The house was built of Florida cypress with lighter pine beams, solid as a ship, on the highest mound, and it had four huge bedrooms and a fireplace.

The second place was an old stilt house built in eight feet of water off a spoil bank near Fleming Key. It had only one small bedroom, but it was open and airy, built of paintless pine clapboard, and it had a bottle-gas stove and refrigerator for cooking, and a rainwater cistern for drinking and washing. But best of all, it had a long porch with water all around.

So it had come down to this final night for me to make my decision. This last December night, two weeks before Christmas. The wind came roaring down from the northland, and clouds went streaming by in the pale winter dusk. The little alcohol stove had warmed the cabin and cooked our supper, and the woman had put coffee on to boil—for afterward. And now, hours later, we lay naked beneath the soft Navy-issue blanket, tired with our loving. Her breasts were exposed above the covers, flattened and round with their own weight, and she sipped at the coffee, sharing it with me.

"Dusky, do you want my advice?" she asked softly in the weak cabin light.

"That and more."

She smiled dreamily, her hair silken on the pillow. "I liked that house on the island. It's so big and private, and you'd have room in case you ever wanted to . . . have someone come and stay with you."

I began to massage her stomach, feeling the warmth of her, and the heat of her thighs.

"That little house built on stilts is too isolated for you, Dusky. It wouldn't be good. You need people."

I rolled her over and began tracing the curve of her back and buttocks with my lips, feeling her legs lift and spread. She moaned softly and whispered, "Dusky, have I helped? With the island, if you ever wanted to marry again, you could . . ."

She said no more, and I didn't answer. She had helped with her advice; helped tremendously.

A week after that good woman Fayette Kunkle returned to Chicago, sweet tears of love in her eyes. I gave the surly old owner of the property a check. He said to keep a close eye on the place during storms. He said the stilt house rocked like a boat . . .

Here's an exciting glimpse of
the thrilling adventure that awaits you in
the next novel of this action-packed series

CUBAN DEATH-LIFT

In a foreign land, a land of aliens and alien politics, the killing becomes easier. The screams still haunt you, but the faces lose shape; dissipate like a sea fog at first light, and you become more and more a stranger— and the shadows become confidants. Separated from the reality of your country, your friends, your home, the newly dead become nothing more than obstacles on a path already followed, like beads on an abacus, or fears that have been conquered, and you know—with a pain like a white cold light—that you must keep killing, you must stay on the path, because it is forever and always the only way back. . . .

The day before my federal connection, Norm Fizer, told me about the disappearance of the three CIA agents in Mariel Harbor, Cuba, the squall hit.

The word "squall" doesn't seem strong enough to describe the storm that came roaring down unannounced from the open ocean of the westnorthwest. Winds gusting to ninety knots, seas walling ten to fifteen feet, death written all over the face of it. And the weather boys in southern Florida did a bad job of picking it up. A damn bad job. For them it meant just one more mistake to log with the others and forget. But for the thousands of Cuban-Americans in small boats bound for Mariel Harbor to pick up relatives in the largest Cuban sea lift in history, it meant disaster.

It was a Sunday in late April. Normally, April is a time for recovery in Key West. The barrage of tourism is over by Easter, and the citizens of the little island city that has become America's chic dead end usually spend April walking the spent streets, blinking their eyes at the new quiet, at the return of the old slowness, like bears just out of hibernation.

But not this April.

You must have heard all about it, headline after headline, with film at eleven. The international newsmongers have turned us all into victims. We've become headline addicts, and they've increased our supply so gradually and steadily that we don't even realize the seriousness of our addiction. Most of us forget the dreams we've just had in the white glare of the morning edition, and at six we're too busy with Cronkite's understated lamentations to hear the words of our own children. The little man from Walden Pond saw the folly of that, but he was no anchorman, so who listens?

So you know about the Cubans who crashed the gate at the Peruvian embassy outside of Havana and demanded political asylum in early April. It was nothing new, really. Cubans tired of Castro's pipe dream had long ago figured out that breaking into the embassies of Peru and Costa Rica was the most reliable way out. But this time the unexpected happened. When the Peruvians, as always, refused to return the would-be refugees, Castro sent bulldozers to crash down the gates, removed his military force, and announced that anyone who wanted to abandon "the dream of socialism" was welcome to take refuge at the little embassy. Within two days, more than ten thousand Cubans had collected on the grounds. There was no food, so they ate the mangoes off the embassy tree, and then the leaves, and then the bark. The embassy's cat and guard dog were killed and roasted over an open fire. By the time the Peruvians—with the help of Costa Rica—had started to airlift refugees (fifty at a time) to South America, the world press got hold of the story, and Castro was made to look like the maniac he is. He might not care a hoot about the needs of his people, but he sure is sensitive to world opinion. He saw the refugees getting off the planes in Costa Rica as the source of his disgrace, so he found a way to halt the airlift—one of his goons pushed a Costa Rican diplomat through a plate-glass window. It wasn't an admirable method of diplomacy, but it was effective. The airlift was halted immediately. Then Castro did something which at the time seemed even stranger. He let it be known that if Americans wanted to come to Cuba by boat, they were welcome to pick up relatives—whether they were among the thousands at the Peruvian embassy or not. At first it didn't make any sense. I followed the news reports, like everyone else in Key West, and couldn't figure it out. Why would Castro suddenly give his people the freedom of choice? And then I remembered something my little friend Carlos de Marti had told me. Carlos is in love with a Cuban woman—whom he had grown up with before his parents shipped him off to America in 1960. Once a month—if he can manage it—Carlos makes the dangerous ninety-mile crossing alone to visit his girl on a secluded beach, and then sneaks back, bringing with him two cases of Hatuey beer for me. After his last trip, he had told me the way things were in Cuba.

"Very bad, *amigo*," he had said. As always, he had brought the beer down to the docks at Garrison Bight in Key West where I moor my charter boat, *Sniper*. "My little love asked me if, on my next trip, I would consider bringing her and her family back. That is the only thing that keeps us apart—her family. But things are very bad there now and getting worse. Little bugs ruined the national sugarcane crop, and there is some blue fungus that has killed all the tobacco. At first it was a joke, see? No tobacco, so Fidel could no longer smoke his big Cohiva cigars. But then it was not so funny. There was no money, so there was no food. When starving people are caught stealing oranges from the national groves, they were imprisoned. My little love has gotten so thin, *amigo*, that I am worried. The next trip, she will come back with me—family or no family."

When I remembered that, it started to make more sense. American boats in Cuba would bring American dollars. And unloading poor Cubans would take some pressure off Castro's economy.

When the first two boatloads of refugees came into Key West on April 21, I understood even further. I was out off Mule Key at the time, trying to chum up some bonefish for two doctors from Moline. The first boats back were two Miami lobster fishermen—the *Dos Hermanos* and the *Blanchie III*. I watched the Coast Guard escort them back to the submarine base beside the low, dun-colored geometrics of old Fort Taylor. The boats were pathetically overloaded. One of Castro's little jokes. Overload the American boats just to see how many would be lost on the dangerous crossing of the Florida Strait. And for all the people on those two boats, there weren't that many relatives of Cuban-Americans. For every three relatives Castro allowed to leave, he sent about twenty of his castoffs—the elderly, political prisoners, habitual criminals. Another of his little jokes. But the Cuban-Americans didn't care—and I couldn't blame them. Most of them still had mothers, fathers, sisters, and brothers back in Cuba and it was their only chance to get them out. So they filed into Key West, thousands upon thousands, trailering their small fishing boats behind their cars, gas in plastic cans, food in coolers, ready to risk their lives to make the crossing and get their loved ones back. There wasn't enough hotel space on the island, so they slept in their cars and drank their morning coffee sitting on the curbs of sidewalks.

Yes, it was a strange April in Key West.

There were so many Cuban-Americans unloading their boats at Garrison Bight that the Sheriff's Department had to send deputies to direct traffic day and night. And the little harbor was packed. For those of us who had boats on charterboat row, it was a real pain in the butt. Most of them had little knowledge of seamanship, so they were constantly running over anchorlines and ramming into wharves and other boats, occasionally catching fire. It was a deadly serious kind of Keystone Kops. It got so that the other guides and I were afraid to leave our boats unguarded. When you came in from a charter, there were normally two or three Cuban-American boats in your slip, and it wasn't easy getting them to move. There were people and noise and traffic everywhere, so finally I just said to hell with it.

And that's how I happened to be out in my stilt house off Calda Bank when the squall hit.

It's some kind of place to watch a squall come in. It's an old fisherman's shack, built in open water eight feet deep, and the nearest land is Fleming Key—about a mile or so away. The old pine clapboard is a weathered gray, and the roof is tin. The sixteen pilings it's built on are stout and smell of creosote, and they angle down into the clear water where barracuda hang in the shadows and big gray snapper swim their nervous figure eights. I had bought the stilt house only a few months before. I wanted solitude, and I had the money—more money than I could use in a lifetime, after that deadly last mission off the Marquesas. I had plenty to forget, and I was tired of the strange April madness that had overtaken Key West.

I wanted to be alone, to rest, to forget. And

there is no place on earth better for being alone than a stilt house.

On the Friday before the squall, I ambled up to the marina at Garrison Bight and told Stevie Wise to cancel all my charters until the craziness was over. Stevie looked harried and weary, which isn't hard to understand, really. He lives on an old lunker of a houseboat named *Fred Astaire,* which is as famous around Key West for its parties as Stevie is well known for his enthusiastic bachelorhood. But it was neither women nor parties which had exhausted him. It was the madness of what the newspapers were calling the Freedom Flotilla.

We stood in the little marina office staring out at the wild activity in the harbor. Cars with boats on trailers sat in a long line down Roosevelt Boulevard, waiting in the April heat to unload at the cement ramp. Fifty or sixty other boats were rafted in the harbor, while others tried to anchor with knotted lines, old engines smoking, their skippers screaming Spanish insults at each other.

"I can't believe they're letting this crap go on," Stevie said. He had taken the phone off the hook to stop the endless barrage of calls he had been getting from the country's news media, and he sat behind the counter on a wooden stool.

"Come on, Stevie—you'd be going too if you had relatives trapped in Cuba."

"No, it's not that." He brushed at his thick black hair with a free hand. With the other, he toyed with a pencil. "What I can't believe is that they're letting those poor people head across the Strait in those damn little boats. Look out there! What are they, mostly eighteen-to-twenty-three-footers? Shit, that's suicide."

"You've got to admire their bravery. They're a determined people."

"Yeah, determined to get themselves killed. I don't see why they all just don't hire shrimp boats—or licensed captains like you—to take them across. Makes a helluva lot more sense."

"Stevie, you know what those shrimp-boat people are charging—and if you don't, you ought to walk on down and have a beer at the Kangaroo's Pouch. That's where all the dealing's going on. The shrimp boats are getting between fifty and a hundred thou in cash for a trip. And that's in advance—with no guarantees. And the reason I'm not going is that no one I know has asked. The Cuban-Americans I do know are close friends, and I suppose they just don't want to put me on the spot."

"And what if they did ask?"

I thought for a moment. Would I go? Castro was making a fool of everyone who went to Mariel Harbor, no doubt about that. He was making a fool of Americans, his own people—everyone but himself. But the bottom line was that there were good people who looked upon this sea lift as their only chance to rescue their relatives from Castro's little commie paradise. Some paradise.

Stevie stared at me with his mocking brown eyes and began to grin. "If one of your friends asked, you'd be gone in a minute, MacMorgan. You know it's true."

I snorted. Maybe it was. And maybe that's why

I had decided to isolate myself on my stilt house—
to escape being asked. I didn't want to haul
Castro's castoffs, so I was taking the coward's way
out. You don't have to make any decisions when
the world can't find you. And I was tired of decisions. I wanted to sit in my little weather-scoured
shack on the sea, drink cold beer, read good
books, and catch fish—just to let them go and
watch them swim free again. Key West could have
its traffic and its Mariel Harbor madness. And it
could have it without me.

I finished rescheduling my charters, shoved the
long black calendar back under the counter, and
turned to leave. As I did, Stevie stopped me.

"Hey, Dusky—I almost forgot." He began shuf-
fling through a stack of papers on a metal spindle.
"You got a message here someplace. . . ."

"It'll keep."

"Naw, the guy said it was very important. Had
nothing to do with a charter—hey, here it is."

I took the narrow envelope he handed me and
opened it. It was from Norm Fizer. Stormin' Norman we had called him on one very secret mission
a long, long time ago back in Cambodia. I had
been a Navy SEAL back then, more fish than man,
more killer than fish. It was a dirty, nasty, dangerous time, but I had come to respect and admire
Fizer during our mission there. He's a fed—and
one of the rare good ones. I owed him a lot—
and not just because of Cambodia. When the drug
runners—the pirates who roam the Florida Strait
and call Key West home—made the mistake of
murdering my family and my best friend, Norm
had seen to it that I had the chance to get even. He

had hired me as a government freelance trouble-shooter, working outside the law to expedite the work of the lawkeepers.

The note read:

> Dusky,
> Wanted to congratulate you again on the Marquesas affair. Well done. May have something else for you. Since you moved off *Sniper*, I don't know where you are staying so it is important you call me at the Atlanta number as soon as possible.
>
> NF

It was typed in plain block pica, just typed initials for a signature. So it was business. But I wasn't ready for any more business. Not now, anyway. I had been having a bad time of it since that brutal night off the little chain of mangrove islands called the Marquesas. At night I couldn't sleep, and during the day I couldn't seem to wake up. I was drinking too much beer, and my hands shook slightly when I tied new leaders. That's what killing does to you. It steals into the middle of your brain and begins to eat its way out again. I needed more time to shake it, to put it all behind me, to crush the nightmares in the peace of isolation.

I crumpled the note and jammed it into the pocket of my khaki fishing shorts.

"You never gave me this."

"What? Huh?" Stevie had a swatter in his hand, and he was swinging at a luminous deerfly that buzzed its complaints about the invention of glass windows.

"Do me a favor, Stevie, and play along."

He gave me an unconcerned shrug. "Captain MacMorgan hasn't been in today, sir. Sorry, I don't know where he's living."

Outside, I nudged my thirty-four-foot sport-fisherman out of her berth, feeling the sweet sync of her twin 453 GMC diesels bubbling me over the clear green water of the harbor. I had an icy Hatuey beer in a Styrofoam hand-cooler, a pinch of Copenhagen snuff wry in my lower lip, and as I piloted from the flybridge, I tried to recapture the delight I usually felt in going out to sea alone.

But it didn't work. I couldn't get the muscles in my shoulders to relax, and it seemed as if I looked out onto the world, through glazed eyes. I dropped *Sniper* into dead idle as I came up behind four ratty fiberglass fishing boats loaded with gas cans, boxes of food, and determined Cuban-Americans, all heading out Garrison Bight Channel, bound for the wicked Florida Straits. The guy running the point boat couldn't have been more than eighteen. He had a tired outboard, belching smoke as it struggled to push the little skiff onward. The kid was shirtless, there was a smile on his face. But in the depths of my despair, it seemed as though a raven-shaped shadow haloed his head, diving and soaring, and the shadow was death. . . .

SIGNET

Randy Wayne White
writing as Randy Striker

"Raises the bar of the action thriller."
—Miami Herald

KEY WEST CONNECTION

Ex-Navy SEAL Dusky MacMorgan survived a military hell only to find it again where he least expects it—as a fisherman trolling the Gulf stream in his thirty-foot clipper. His new life is shattered when a psychotic pack of drug runners turns the turquoise waters red with the blood of his beloved family. Armed with an arsenal so hot it could blow the Florida coast sky-high, he's tracking the goons responsible—right into the intimate circle of a corrupt U.S. senator living beyond the law in his own island fortress. But now it has to withstand the force of a one-man hit-squad.

0-451-21801-9

Available wherever books are sold or at
www.penguin.com